BELLAROO CREEK

Three brave women, three strong men...and one town on the brink

Bellaroo Creek in the Australian Outback is a town in need of rescue! So the arrival of three single women and a few adorable kids is exactly the injection of life it needs. Are the town and its ruggedly gorgeous cattleman prepared for the adventure ahead?

One town, three heart-warming romances to cherish forever!

The Cattleman's Ready-Made Family by Michelle Douglas
in July 2013

Miracle in Bellaroo Creek by Barbara Hannay
in August 2013

Patchwork Family in the Outback by Soraya Lane
in September 2013

MICHELLE DOUGLAS

The Cattleman's Ready-Made Family

BELLAROO CREEK

HARLEQUIN ROMANCE

Recycling programs
for this product may
not exist in your area.

ISBN-13: 978-0-373-74250-9

THE CATTLEMAN'S READY-MADE FAMILY

First North American Publication 2013

Copyright © 2013 by Michelle Douglas

This edition published by arrangement with Harlequin Books S.A.

For questions and comments about the quality of this book, please contact us at CustomerService@Harlequin.com.

Printed in U.S.A.

At the age of eight **Michelle Douglas** was asked what she wanted to be when she grew up. She answered, "A writer." Years later she read an article about romance writing and thought, *Ooh, that'll be fun.* She was right. When she's not writing, she can usually be found with her nose buried in a book. She is currently enrolled in an English master's program for the sole purpose of indulging her reading and writing habits further. She lives in a leafy suburb of Newcastle, on Australia's east coast, with her own romantic hero—husband Greg, who is the inspiration behind all her happy endings.

Michelle would love you to visit her at her website, www.michelle-douglas.com.

Recent books by Michelle Douglas

FIRST COMES BABY...
THE NANNY WHO SAVED CHRISTMAS
BELLA'S IMPOSSIBLE BOSS
THE MAN WHO SAW HER BEAUTY
THE SECRETARY'S SECRET
CHRISTMAS AT CANDLEBARK FARM
THE CATTLEMAN, THE BABY AND ME

Other titles by this author available in ebook format.

To the Valley Girls for the support,
the laughter and the champagne.

CHAPTER ONE

ARE YOU LOOKING FOR A TREE CHANGE?
Do you long for fresh air and birdsong?
Do you relish fresh-picked produce?
Do you hunger for a gentler pace of life?
RENT A FARMHOUSE FOR $1 A WEEK!
If you're a community-minded family, why not
rent a farmhouse for $1 a week in beautiful
Bellaroo Creek?
We can promise you a fresh start and genuine
country hospitality.

CAMERON MANNING PACED from the fence to the empty farmhouse and back again. He checked his watch. The second hand hadn't moved much from the last time he'd looked. With a curse, he threw himself down on the bench, squatting beneath one of the Kurrajong trees that screened this farmhouse from the rest of his property, and drummed his fingers against his thigh.

Where was the woman?

The slats of the bench, badly in need of a nail or ten, bit into his back. It would've been more comfortable to sit on the veranda, but here the deep shade screened him. It'd give him a chance to contemplate his new tenants unobserved.

He scowled. If they ever turned up.

To be honest, he didn't much care if they did or not. All he wanted was Tess Laing's signature on his contract so he could hightail it out of here again. He had work to do. Serious work.

He leaned forward, steepling his hands under his chin as he glared at the farmhouse. Now that he had the cattle station on the western edges of his property sorted and in the capable hands of an under-manager, and he and station manager Fraser had dealt with all that needed overseeing for the operation of the sheep station and the planting and harvesting of the wheat crop, the only item left remaining was the canola contract.

He needed that locked in.

Once it was he'd be free to leave this godforsaken place. He'd shake off the dust of the poisonous memories that not only plagued his dreams at night but his waking hours too.

He leapt up, a familiar bitterness coating his tongue and the blackness of betrayal settling over him like a straitjacket. For the first time in his life he understood his father's retreat from the world.

He recognised the same impulse in himself now. He gritted his teeth. He would *not* give into it.

Blasting out a breath, he glanced at his watch. 3:30 p.m. The woman had said she'd arrive somewhere between two and three o'clock. He slashed a hand through the air. Lucky she wasn't an employee.

Lucky for her, that was. He could fire an employee. He wrenched his gaze from the forty hectares of lovingly improved land that stretched out behind the farmhouse. Land he'd spent the last two years painstakingly improving—turning the soil, digging out rocks, fertilising…backbreaking work. And now…

He seized the contract he'd tossed onto the bench, rolled it up and slapped it against his legs. Once it was signed he could shake the dust of Bellaroo Creek from his feet for good. After that, his mother could deal with the new tenants.

And good luck to them.

He paced some more. He threw himself back to the bench and kept his gaze firmly fixed on the road and not on those contentious forty hectares. Finally a car appeared at the end of the gravel road, moving slowly—a big, solid station wagon.

Cam didn't move from his spot in the shade, not even stirring when the breeze sent a light branch dancing across his hair, but every muscle in his body tightened. He dragged in a breath and counselled patience. He would explain the inadvertent mix-up to

Tess Laing. He would *patiently* explain that a mistake had somehow seen his forty hectares included in her lease on the house. He would get her signature to turn those forty hectares back over to him. End of story.

If the mix-up had been inadvertent—an *honest* mistake. Bile burned his throat. Honesty and his family didn't necessarily go hand in hand. He expected betrayal from Lance. His nostrils flared and his lips thinned. He would never underestimate his little brother's treacherous resentment again. He would never again trust a word that spilled from Lance's forked tongue. But his mother, had she…?

An invisible hand tried to squeeze the air out of his lungs, but he ignored it to thrust out his jaw. Mistake or not, he needed that land. And he *would* get it back. He'd talk this woman out of whatever ridiculous hobby farm idea she'd come out here with. He'd offer her a fair price to lease the land back. He'd make whatever bargain he needed to. His hand curled around the contract. Once he had her signature, Kurrajong Station's obligations would be met. And he'd be free to head off for the far horizons of Africa.

Lance, Fiona and his mother could sink or swim on their own.

The car finally reached the farmhouse and pulled to a halt. He rested his elbows on his knees, eyes narrowed. Would she be some hard-nosed business type or a free-spirited hippy?

Three car doors were flung open and three passengers shot out from the car's interior like bottled fizzy water that had been shaken and then opened— a woman and two children. All of them raced around to the front of the car and bounced from one foot to the other as if they'd been cooped up for too long.

He studied the woman. She didn't look like a hard-nosed businesswoman. She didn't look like a nature-loving hippy either. She looked…

In her red-and-black tartan skirt, thick black tights and black Doc Martens she reminded him of a ladybird. Her movements, though, were pure willy wagtail—light, graceful…cheeky. In fact, she looked like a university student. He sat up straighter. She couldn't be old enough to have two kids!

He turned his attention to the children—a boy of around seven and a girl a year or two younger. He had a vague recollection of his mother mentioning their ages as being a real coup for the school. It was the main reason the committee had chosen this family from the flood of applicants.

A frown built inside him. They might be a coup for the school, but right now they were a disaster for him.

Finally he allowed himself a grim smile as the woman shook out her arms and legs as if she'd spent too many hours in the car—granted it was a bit of a hike from Sydney to Bellaroo Creek—and then moved to rest her hands on the front fence, a child standing either side of her. Her dark hair shone in the autumn sun. It made him realise how brightly the sun shone in the soft autumn stillness of the afternoon.

The boy glanced up at her, indecision flitting across his face. 'What do you think?' He glanced back at the cottage. 'Did you know it would look like this?'

Cam pursed his lips at the edge of disappointment lacing the boy's words. The little girl moved closer to the woman as if seeking reassurance. Cam straightened. If they hated the place they'd happily sign the whole kit and caboodle back over to him! That'd solve everything.

'I had no idea what it'd look like.'

Her voice sounded like music.

She beamed down at the children and then clasped her hands beneath her chin. 'Oh, but I think it's perfect!' She knelt on the ground, heedless of the danger to her tights, to put an arm about each of them.

The little girl pressed in against her. 'Really?'

'You do?' The little boy leaned against her too.

'Oh, yes!'

Cam wondered where she came by such confidence and enthusiasm. She was from the city. What did she know about country living?

Unless she'd known about those forty hectares

before times and knew of their value. Unless Lance had already got to her, somehow. Unless—

'Look at the size of the yard. Just think how perfect it'll be once we've mown the lawn and trimmed back that hedge of...' She gestured with her head because it was obvious she didn't want to let go of either child.

'You don't know what it is,' the boy accused.

'I have no idea,' she agreed with one of the widest grins Cam had ever seen.

Plumbago. He could've told her, but something hard and heavy had settled in his stomach. He could've at least mown the lawn for them, couldn't he? He might've been flat out with organising the cattle station, the wheat crop and mustering sheep, but he should've found the time to manage at least that much. He mightn't want these new tenants—his mother had manipulated him superbly on that front—but that wasn't this woman's fault, or her children's.

'But won't it be fun finding out?'

'I guess.'

'And just imagine how pretty the cottage will look once we've painted it.'

She was going to paint his cottage?

'Pink!'

'Blue!'

'Cream!' She grinned back at the kids. 'We'll draw straws.'

He hoped she rigged that one.

The little girl started to jump up and down. 'We can have chickens!'

'And a dog!' The little boy started to jump too.

'And a lemon tree and pretty curtains at the window.' The woman laughed, bouncing back upright. 'And…?'

'And we'll all live happily ever after,' they hollered together in a chorus, and Cam found he couldn't drag his eyes from them.

It was just a house on an average acre block. But it hit him then what this property represented. A new start. And he knew exactly what that meant.

With everything in his soul.

The woman clapped her hands, claiming his attention once more. 'I think we should sing our song to our new perfect home.'

And they started to sing. The children held a wobbly melody and the woman harmonised, and they so loved their song and grinned so madly at each other that Cam found his lips lifting upwards.

'The house loves us now,' the little girl whispered.

'I believe you're right.'

'I love a veranda,' the little boy said and Cam knew it was his way of saying he approved of the house…of their new start.

The woman smiled *that* smile again and Cam had to shift on his bench. 'Right,' she said, dusting off her hands, 'what we need now is the key.'

That was his cue.

He hadn't meant to sit here for so long watching them without declaring himself. He'd only thought—hoped—that a moment's observation would give him the measure of his new tenants. Except... He found himself more confounded than ever.

'That'd be where I come in.'

Both children literally jumped out of their skins at his abrupt declaration and he found himself wishing he'd cleared his throat first to give them warning of his presence.

The little girl ducked behind the woman, her hands clutching fistfuls of the woman's shirt. The boy wavered for a moment or two and then moved in front of the woman, face pale and hands clenched, but obviously determined to protect her. It was a simple act of courage that knocked Cam sideways. His heart started to pound.

The woman reached out and tousled the boy's hair and pulled him back in against her. She kept her voice solidly cheerful. 'Aha! You'll be our emissary from the town.'

Not quite, but... 'I have your key.'

'Good Lord!' She planted her hands on her hips as he emerged more fully into the sunlight. 'Look at the size of you. I bet you're a big help to your mum.'

And beside her both children immediately relaxed, and he found himself careful to keep the smile on his face and to move towards them slowly. 'Actually, I guess I'm your landlord. I'm Cameron Manning.'

She frowned. 'I thought Lorraine…'

'My mother.'

'Ah.' She nodded, and then a cheeky grin peeked out. 'The mother you're such a big help to, no doubt.'

Actually, there was every doubt in the world on that head.

'I'm Tess, and this is Tyler and Kristina—Ty and Krissie for short—and we're very pleased to meet you.'

She held out her hand and he moved the final few feet forward to shake it. With such dark hair—nearly black—he'd thought she'd be pale but she had skin the colour of deep golden honey. Her palm slid against his, smooth and cool. Large brown eyes surveyed him with undisguised intensity as if attempting to sum up the man beneath the bulk. She smelled of liquorice and cool days, and when he finally stepped back Cam found his heart pounding.

'Can you ride a horse?' Tyler asked, awe stretching through his voice.

'I can.'

'I want to be a cowboy when I grow up.'

'Then you've come to the right town,' Cam said, though he could hardly believe that he spoke them. He hadn't meant to be so welcoming. He'd meant to be businesslike and brisk. But that boy had stepped in front of his mother when he'd thought she'd needed protecting. There were grown men who were afraid to take Cam on physically. At six feet three and sporting the kind of muscles that hard work on the land developed, he understood that reluctance.

He was big and he was strong. Yet, still, this little boy had faced his fear and Cam couldn't ignore that.

'Auntie Tess—' the little girl tugged on the woman's sleeve '—I've gotta go.'

Auntie? She wasn't their mother?

'Right.' She stared at him expectantly. 'The key?'

He recalled how he'd considered talking them out of this property. The contract he'd left sitting on the bench fluttered in the breeze. He considered Tyler's act of courage and Krissie's excitement about chickens and the way Tess had quieted the children's fears with a song.

A new start. He knew all about the need for those.

He fished the key out of his pocket and handed it over.

The three of them raced to the front door of the old farmhouse. Cam retrieved his contract and then stood under the Kurrajong tree and dragged in a breath. Okay, the house was neither here nor there. He had no plans for it. Those forty hectares, though, did matter and he wanted—needed—Tess's signature on the dotted line.

And he wasn't leaving until he had it.

He followed them into the house.

'Bags this room!' Tyler shouted from the corridor off to the right. 'It has a view of the front and I can see who's coming, which is good 'cause I'm the man of the house.'

That almost made Cam smile again, only he remembered how pale the boy had gone when Cam had appeared unannounced.

The toilet flushed, the sound of water running in a tap and then Krissie raced down the corridor too. 'Auntie Tess, this is your room! And this one is mine 'cause it's right next to yours!'

Cam let out a breath as he glanced around. The yard might need some TLC, but the women from the Save-Our-Town committee had cleaned this place to within an inch of its life. The furniture might be mismatched—favouring comfort more than elegance—but there wasn't a single dust bunny in sight. 'Coffee?' he called out, wanting Tess to know he'd followed them into the house.

'Excellent idea,' she called back.

He strode into the kitchen and put the jug on to boil. The farmhouse wasn't fancy by any means, but it had a certain homey charm. He had the impression that Tess would turn it into a home in the blink of an eye.

What on earth was he talking about? He shook his head. She already had, and he wasn't sure how. It took more than a smile and a song to make a home.

Didn't it?

He let himself out of the back door, the contract

burning a hole against his palm as he moved down the steps to stare out at those magical forty hectares. She was paying a dollar a week in rent for all that. It was enough to make a grown man weep.

He straightened. He had a canola contract to fulfil—he'd given his word—and he wasn't going to let anyone steal it out from under him. His lips twisted. He didn't doubt for a moment that one person in particular in Bellaroo Creek would try to do exactly that, but would his mother be party to such duplicity?

'You better get that particular look off your face quick smart or you'll give Ty and Krissie nightmares for a month.'

He blinked to find Tess holding a mug out to him. He frowned. 'I was supposed to be making those.' He'd meant to make a stab at the country-hospitality approach first before bombarding her with his demand. Besides, she had dark circles beneath those magnificent eyes of hers. If she'd left two hours from the other side of Sydney this morning she'd have driven for the best part of eight hours.

The least he could've done was make her a cup of coffee. And mow the lawn. And trim that hedge of plumbago.

'No matter, and sorry but I put milk in it before I thought. If you want sugar—'

'No, this is great,' he said hastily. 'Thanks.'

Her lips twitched. 'You didn't strike me as a sugar-in-their-coffee type.'

What was that supposed to mean?

She stared out at the fields and drew a breath deep into her lungs. 'Oh, my, look at it all!'

His skin tightened. His muscles tensed.

'You live in a beautiful part of the world, Cameron.'

'Cam.' The correction came out husky. The only person to call him Cameron was his mother. 'But you're right.' He nodded towards the fields. 'It's beautiful.'

And by rights it should be his. He spun to her. 'There's something—'

'I want to apologise for being late.'

He blinked at her interruption. 'No problem.'

'We had one threat of car sickness.'

He grimaced.

'And I took a wrong turn when we left Parkes. I started heading towards Trundle instead of Bella-roo Creek.'

'That's in completely the opposite direction.'

'That's what a man on a tractor told us.'

He shifted his weight, opened his mouth.

She pointed back behind her with an infectious grin. 'Do you know somebody left us a cake?'

He found one side of his mouth hitching up at her delight. 'That'd be my mother. I'd know her sultana cake anywhere. It's her speciality.'

'Then you must stay for a slice.'

He adjusted his stance. 'Look, there's something I need to talk to you about.'

Her gaze had dropped to take an inventory of his shoulders and he could feel himself tensing up again, but at his words her eyes lifted. She sipped her coffee. 'Yes?'

'It's about that land out there.' He gestured out in front of them.

'Wow! Look how big the yard is!'

With whoops, Ty and Krissie swooped down the back steps and into the yard. Cam winced at how overgrown it all was.

'What kind of tree is that, Auntie Tess?'

She shaded her eyes and peered to where Krissie pointed. 'Tell me?' she shot out of the corner of her mouth and it made him want to laugh. 'Please?'

'Lemon tree,' he answered in an undertone.

She turned and beamed at him. It cracked open something wide inside him—something that made him hot and cold at the same time. Before he could react in any way whatsoever, she set her coffee to the ground, danced down to the lemon tree and the children with her arms outstretched as if to embrace them all. But he could've sworn she'd whispered, 'Smile,' at him before she'd danced away.

'It's a lemon tree!'

The children cheered. They all started rattling off the things they'd make with the lemons—lemonade, lemon butter, lemon-meringue pie, lemon chicken, lemon tea—as if it were a litany they'd learned off by heart. As if it were a list that made the world a better place.

And as he watched them Cam thought that maybe it did.

'Where do you live, um…Mr…?'

He gazed down at Krissie with her blonde curls, and her big brown eyes identical to Tess's, and recalled the way she'd jumped when he'd first spoken. *Smile.* 'You can call me Cam,' he said, making his voice gentle. 'If that's okay with your auntie Tess.'

Tess nodded her assent, but he was aware that she watched him like a hawk—or a mother bear hell-bent on protecting her cubs.

'You can see my house from here.' He led them towards the line of Kurrajong trees at the side fence and gestured across the acre field to his home beyond.

'Wow,' Ty breathed. 'It's big.'

It was, and the sandstone homestead was a point of local pride. 'My great-great-great-grandfather was one of the first settlers in the area. His son built that house.'

'Is it a farm?'

'It is. It's called Kurrajong Station because of all the Kurrajong trees. It's large for these parts at six thousand hectares.' It wasn't a boast, just pure fact.

'What do you farm?'

That was Tess. He eyed her for a moment. He sure as hell hoped she didn't have any interests in that direction. 'Cattle, sheep and wheat mostly.' And just as soon as he had his forty hectares back he'd be branching out into canola. Diversification would ensure Kurrajong's future. And once that was all in place, he could leave.

For good.

'Are we allowed to play in that field?'

Ty glanced up at him hopefully. Cam bit back a sigh. He didn't have anything against the Save-Our-Town scheme in principle. He mightn't want to live in Bellaroo Creek any longer, but his station's prosperity did, to some extent, hinge on the town's ongoing existence. It was just that in practical terms...

So much for his jealously guarded privacy.

Still, they were just kids. They wouldn't disturb his peace too much. And kids would be kids—they'd want to explore, kick balls, run. Besides, he sensed that these kids needed more kindness than most. Rather than declare the paddock out of bounds, he found himself saying, 'You'd better wait till you've made friends with my dog first.'

Ty's face lit up. 'You have a dog? When can we meet him?'

Cam shoved his hands in his pockets and glanced at Tess. 'Tomorrow?'

She nodded. 'Excellent.'

Her cap of dark hair glowed in the sun and her

eyes were bigger than they had any right to be. He gave himself a mental kick and turned back to the kids. 'I want you both to promise me something. If you see a paddock with either cows or big machinery in it, promise you won't go into it. It could be dangerous.'

They gazed up at him with eyes too solemn for their age and nodded.

Lord, he didn't mean to frighten them. *Smile!* 'We just want to make sure you stay safe, okay?'

They nodded again.

'And you shouldn't go outside your own yard or this paddock without letting your auntie Tess know first.'

Tess watched Cam as he talked with the children. His initial gruffness apparently hid a natural gentleness for all those smaller than him. Not that there'd be too many who'd be larger! The longer she watched, the more aware she became of the warmth stealing over her.

She shook it off. She wanted this move to be perfect. She wanted to believe that everyone in Bellaroo Creek would have Ty and Krissie's best interests at heart. She wasn't going to let that hope lead her astray, though. Too much depended on her making the right decisions. She swallowed, her heart still burning at the children's reactions when Cam had startled them—their instinctive fear and suspicion.

She gripped her hands together. Please, please, please let moving to Bellaroo Creek be the right decision. Please, please, please let the children learn to trust again. Please, God, help her make them feel secure and safe, loved.

She relaxed her hands and crossed her fingers. After the initial shaky start, it certainly looked as if the kids had taken to their laconic neighbour. After all, not only did he know how to ride a horse, but he had a dog too. True hero material.

Her gaze drifted down his denim-clad legs and a long slow sigh built up inside her. He could certainly fill out a pair of jeans nicely. With cheeks suddenly burning, she wrenched her gaze away. For heaven's sake, she hadn't moved to Bellaroo Creek for that kind of fresh start!

Besides—she glanced up at him through her lashes—Cameron Manning was a man with something on his mind. She'd sensed it the moment he'd stepped out of the shadows of the trees. She had relaxed a little, though, when he'd handed over the key. She had no intention of handing it back. She'd signed a legally binding lease. She'd paid the first year's rent up front. All fifty-two dollars of it.

The children ran off further down the backyard to explore, but even while she sensed he wanted to talk, she didn't suggest they go inside to do just that. She wanted to keep an eye on Ty and Krissie. She wanted them to know she was nearby. She wanted to share in the joy of their discoveries. She had every intention of smoothing over any little concerns or ripples that threatened their well-being.

That was her first priority. That mattered a million times more than anything else at the moment. Joy, love and hope—that was what these kids needed and that was exactly what they were going to get.

She shot Cam another half-veiled glance. Still, if he was happy to talk out here... 'I—'

'You're their auntie Tess?'

She blinked.

'Where are their parents?'

Ah. She'd thought the entire town would know their story considering she hadn't been reticent about the details in her application. In fact, she'd shamelessly used those details in an attempt to tug on all the unknown heartstrings that would be reading their application.

They walked back towards the house. Tess swooped down to pick up her abandoned coffee from the grass. She chugged back its lukewarm contents and then let the mug dangle loosely from her fingers. 'Why is your surname different from your mother's?'

'I'm the son from her first marriage.'

Right. She nodded towards the children. 'Their father and mother—my sister—died in a car accident three months ago.'

He stilled. 'I'm sorry.'

He sounded genuinely sympathetic and her eyes

started to burn. Even now, three months down the track and a million tears later, she still found condolences hard to deal with. But Cameron's voice sounded low and deep—the tone and breadth midway between an oboe and a cello—and somehow that made it easier. She nodded and kicked herself back into an aimless meandering around the yard.

'Are you interested in farming? In keeping cattle or horses or growing a crop?'

The abrupt change of topic took her off guard. 'God, no!' She hoped he didn't take her horror personally, but she didn't know the first thing about farming. She didn't know much about vegetable gardens or keeping chickens either, she supposed, but she could learn. 'Why?'

'Because there's been a bit of a mix-up with the tenancy agreement.'

Her blood chilled. Just like that. In an instant. Her toes and fingers froze rigid. He couldn't kick them out! *He'd given them the key.*

The children loved this place. *She'd* made sure they'd fallen in love with it—had used her enthusiasm and assumed confidence to give it all a magical promise. Ty and Krissie weren't resilient enough to deal with another disappointment.

And they didn't deserve to.

'I mean, yes,' she snapped out as quickly as she could. 'Farming is exactly the reason we're out here.'

He frowned. In fact, it might be described as a

scowl. But then he glanced at the kids and it became just a frown again. 'I beg your pardon?'

She didn't like the barely leashed control stretching through his voice, but he was not kicking them out. 'What I'm trying to say is that I'm fully prepared to learn farming if that's part of my contract.'

She'd gone over the contract with a fine-tooth comb. She'd consulted a solicitor. Her chin lifted. She'd signed a legally binding contract. She *had* understood it. The solicitor had ensured that. She wasn't in the wrong here. A fine trembling started up in her legs, but she stood her ground. 'I'm not going to let you kick us out.' She even managed to keep her voice perfectly pleasant. 'Just so you know.'

'I don't want to kick you out.'

That was when she knew he was lying. Even though he'd been kind to the children. Even though he'd handed over the key. This man would love it if they left.

Didn't he want to save his town?

By this stage they'd reached the back fence. She set her mug on a fencepost, and then leant against it and folded her arms. 'It's been a long day, Mr Manning, so I'm going to speak plainly.'

He blinked at the formality of her *Mr Manning*. And she saw he understood the sudden distance she'd created between them.

'I signed a contract and I understand my rights. If there's been a mix-up then it hasn't been of my making.' She folded her arms tighter. 'Whatever this mix-up may be, the children and I are not leaving this house. We're living here for the next three years and we're going to carve out a new life for ourselves and we are going to make that work. This is now our home and we're going to make it a good home. Furthermore, you are not going to say anything in front of the children that might upset or alarm them—you hear me?'

His mouth opened and closed. 'I wouldn't dream of it.'

He leaned towards her and he smelled like fresh-cut grass, and it smelled so fresh and young that she wanted to bury her face against his neck and just breathe it in. She shook herself. It'd been a long trip. Very long. 'Then smile!' she snapped.

To her utter astonishment, he laughed, and the grim lines that hooded his eyes and weighed down the corners of his mouth all lightened, and his eyes sparkled, the same deep green as clover.

Her breath caught. The man wasn't just big and broad and a great help to his mum—he was beautiful!

The blood started to thump in a painful pulse about her body. Four months ago she'd have flirted with Cam in an attempt to lighten him up. Three months ago she'd have barely noticed him. It was amazing the changes a single month could bring. One day. In fact, lives could change in a single moment.

And they did.

And they had.

She swallowed. The particular moment that had turned her life on its head might not have been her fault, but if she'd been paying attention she might've been able to avert it. That knowledge would plague her to her grave.

And men, beautiful and otherwise, were completely off the agenda.

She snapped away from him. He frowned. 'Tess, I'm not going to ask you to leave. I swear. This house is all yours for the next three years, and beyond if you want it.'

She bit her lip, glanced back at him. 'Really?'

'Really.'

'Still—' she stuck out a hip '—you're less than enthused about it.'

He hesitated and then shrugged. 'My mother has, in effect, foisted you lot on to me.'

She glanced at the house and then back at him. 'Isn't the house hers?'

'Not precisely.' He exhaled loudly. 'My father made certain provisions for my mother in his will. She has the use of this house along with an attached parcel of land for as long as she lives. When she passes the rights all revert back to the owner of Kurrajong Station.'

'You?'

'Me.'

She pursed her lips. He met her gaze steadily. She wanted to get a handle on this enigmatic neighbour of hers. Was he friend or foe? 'Don't you want to help save Bellaroo Creek?'

'Sure I do.'

'As long as you're not asked to sacrifice too much in the effort, right?'

'As long as I'm not asked to give up a significant portion of my potential income in the process,' he countered.

'How will our being here impact negatively on your income?' Her understanding was that the Save-Our-Town scheme only offered *unused* farmhouses in exchange for ludicrously cheap rents. If their farmhouse was unused he couldn't possibly be losing money. In fact, he'd be fifty-two dollars a year richer.

Her lips suddenly twitched. Cameron Manning didn't strike her as the kind of man who'd stress too much over fifty-two dollars. Not that she needed to stress over money either. It hadn't been the cheap rent but the promise of a fresh start that had lured her out here.

He drew in a breath and then pointed behind her. She turned. 'Forty hectares,' he said. 'Forty hectares I had plans for. Forty hectares my mother had promised to lease to me.'

She slapped a hand to her forehead. 'They were

allotted to me in my tenancy agreement? That's the mix-up you're talking about.'

'Yep.'

'And you want them back?'

'Bingo.'

She laughed in her sudden rush of relief. 'Oh, honey, they're all yours.' What on earth did she want with forty hectares of wide, open space? She had a house and a backyard and a whole ocean of possibilities enough to satisfy her.

She clapped her hands. 'Hey, troops, who's for sultana cake?'

CHAPTER TWO

IT TOOK TESS until her second bite of sultana cake to realise she hadn't allayed her sexy neighbour's concerns.

She stiffened. Umm…not sexy. Taciturn and self-contained, perhaps, and, um… She dragged her gaze from shoulders so broad they made her think of Greek gods and swimsuits and the Mediterranean.

Sleep, rest, peace, that was what she needed. The last month had been a crazy whirlwind and she quite literally hadn't stopped. The two months prior had been a blur of pain and grief.

She flinched at the memory and brushed a hand across her eyes. Bellaroo Creek would bring her the rest and the sleep she craved, but peace? She wasn't sure anything on earth could bring her that.

And she wasn't sure she deserved it.

Cameron hitched an eyebrow. 'A penny for them.'

She stiffened again. Nu-huh. But the exhaustion made her silly—an after-effect of the nonsense she'd used all day to keep the children entertained and in good spirits. 'Are you sure you can afford a penny when I'm only paying you a dollar a week in rent?'

His green eyes gleamed for a tantalizing moment. It made him look younger. She dragged her gaze away and rose. 'I'll just check on the kids. The promise of cake should've had them sprinting inside.'

On cue, the pair came racing through the front door. 'We found a lizard,' Ty announced, breathless with excitement.

'Will it bite us?' Krissie asked, wide-eyed.

She directed the question at Cam. He'd obviously become the source of trusted information. Tess's chest cramped as she stared at them—took in their simple wonder.

'That'll be Old Nelson, the blue-tongue,' Cam said, leaning back in his chair, one long, lean leg stretched out in front of him.

Krissie's eyes widened even further. 'He has a name?'

'Wow, awesome!' Ty breathed. 'Will he bite?'

'Only if you poke him or try to pick him up.'

'Can we take our cake outside, Auntie Tess?'

With a laugh, Tess assented. She watched as they left the room and her chest burned. If only Sarah could see them now. If only—

'You okay?'

She jumped, swung back patting her chest. 'Tired,' she said. She sat and forced a smile. She'd become good at that over the last couple of months—smiling when she didn't feel like it—but she could see it didn't fool Cam. She shrugged. 'They've been through so much, but for this moment they're happy and…and that's no small thing.'

He stared towards the front of the house and then glanced back at her. 'They're great kids, Tess.'

She nodded. 'They really are.' And they deserved so much more than life had dished out to them. Focusing on the negatives wouldn't help anyone, though—least of all Ty and Krissie. She sipped tea. Cam had made a pot while she'd sliced the cake. It was the best tea she'd ever tasted.

She lifted her cup. 'This is seriously good.'

'My mother was the president of the Country Women's Association for a hundred years. Believe me, she made sure her sons knew how to brew a proper pot of tea.'

She made a mental note to join the CWA. But for the moment… 'You want to tell me why you're still so worried about your forty hectares?'

His eyes widened a fraction, but he held her gaze with a steadiness she found disconcerting. 'I had a contract drawn up. I need you to sign it before I can start planting.'

He whipped out a sheaf of papers, literally from thin air as far as her tired brain could tell. He flicked through to the final page and pointed. 'I need your signature here.' He handed her a pen.

She lowered her cup back to its saucer and

dropped her hands to her lap. 'I'm not signing anything I haven't read.'

'Fair enough.' He placed the contract in front of her and leaned back.

'And I'm not reading it now when I'm so tired.'

He frowned.

'And if there's something I don't understand, I'll be consulting my solicitor for clarification.'

He was silent for a long moment and the silence should've sawn on her nerves, but it didn't. After a day of chatter and noise in the confines of the car, the silence was heaven.

'You don't trust me,' he finally said, nodding as if that made perfect sense.

'I don't know you. Once upon a time I'd have been prepared to take spur-of-the-moment risks and trust my gut instincts, but I won't now Tyler and Krissie are in my care.' She leant towards him. 'Are you saying you trust me?' She waved a hand in the direction of the back door and his precious forty hectares. 'By all means start planting tomorrow. I'll keep my word. I'll get the contract back to you by the middle of next week.'

His lips twisted but his eyes danced. 'Nope, don't trust you as far as I could throw you.'

Given his size and the breadth of his shoulders, she had a feeling he could throw her a long way if he so chose.

This time it was he who leaned in towards her,

and that fresh-cut-grass scent danced around her and it was almost as relaxing as silence. 'But I do need to get started on the planting soon if I'm to meet my obligations.'

'I promise not to drag my feet.' She wanted to be on good terms with her neighbours and the townsfolk of Bellaroo Creek. She just had to make sure she didn't risk the children's futures in her eagerness to fit in.

Without thinking, she reached out and touched his hand. He immediately stiffened and she snatched her hand back, her heart suddenly thundering in her ears. 'I, uh… You said you'd bring your dog around to meet the children. Why don't you aim to do that tomorrow morning some time—say, ten o'clock? I'll try and have your contract read by then.'

'If you need more time…'

Her pulse rate refused to slow. 'No, no, it's obvious that time is of the essence. Besides, the kids will no doubt be up early and we have a midday meet-and-greet luncheon at the community hall, so I should have plenty of time in the morning to go over this contract of yours.'

He rose in one swift motion. 'I'll see you at ten.' And then he was gone.

She heard him say goodbye to the children. She supposed she should've followed him to the door to wave him off, but the strength had leached from her legs and she found herself momentarily incapable of even rising from her chair. She'd spent nearly ten hours in the car today. She was dog-tired. She'd just turned her entire life on its head—hers and the children's. And if this move didn't work out…

She shook that thought off. This move had to work out. In the meantime, she refused to allow her sexy neighbour to unsettle her.

She frowned. He *wasn't* sexy.

She glanced at her empty plate, and then at Cam's and realised he hadn't touched his cake—he hadn't even broken off the tiniest corner. She hadn't been hungry for the last three months—ever since she'd received the phone call informing her of Sarah's car accident. But now…

She stared at the cake. She pulled the plate towards her and then poured another cup of tea. She devoured both, slowly, relishing every single delicious mouthful.

The children made instant friends with Boomer, Cam's border collie.

'Will he fetch a ball?' Ty asked, pulling a tennis ball from his pocket.

Cam's mouth angled up in a lopsided smile as he surveyed Ty and Krissie and their barely concealed eagerness. 'Believe me, he'll fetch for longer than you'll be prepared to throw.' With whoops of delight, the children raced around the backyard with Boomer at their heels.

He had a way of smiling at her kids—and, yes, somewhere in the last month she'd started thinking of them as hers—that could melt a woman where she stood. 'Morning,' he finally said, the green of his eyes strangely undiluted in the mid-morning sun.

'It will be,' she countered, 'if you'll teach me the trick to making a perfect pot of tea.'

He laughed and it was only then she saw that while his eyes might be the purest of greens, shadows lurked in their depths. Shadows momentarily dispelled when he laughed.

He followed her into the kitchen. 'One demonstration coming up.'

He should laugh more often. 'Jug's just boiled,' she said, shaking the odd thought aside. Cam might well laugh a hundred times every single day for all she knew.

'Did you fill the jug using hot or cold water?'

'Hot. It makes it come to the boil faster.'

'There's your first mistake.' He poured the contents of the jug down the sink and refilled it from the cold tap. 'Cold water has more oxygen than hot. That's key for the perfect cuppa.'

She sat and stared. 'Well, who'd have known that?' Other than a chemistry professor. And a president of the CWA…and her sons.

He sat too, his eyes twinkling for the briefest of moments. 'It's important to be properly trained in country ways.'

'I never doubted it for a moment.' She leapt up to glance out of the kitchen window to make sure the children were okay. When she swung back she could've sworn he'd been checking out her backside.

His gaze slid away. Her heart thumped. She'd imagined it. She must've imagined it. She frowned, scratched a hand through her hair and tried to think of something to say.

'Did you get a chance to read the contract?'

Of course she'd imagined it, but the shadows were back in his eyes with a vengeance and it left a bitter taste in her mouth, though for the life of her she couldn't explain why. 'Yes.' She took her seat again.

'And?'

The contract had been remarkably straightforward. It hadn't asked her to give up her firstborn or sign her rights away to the house and the acre block it stood on. It simply requested she sign over the attached forty hectares of land and to waive her rights to any profits he accrued from the use of the land. Except...

On the table, one of his hands tightened. 'You have a problem?'

She hauled in a breath and nodded. 'I do.'

'You want more money for the lease?'

She hated the derisive light that entered his eyes. She pushed the contract towards him. 'I made my amendment in black ink. That's what I'm prepared to sign.'

Blowing out a breath, he pulled the contract towards him and flipped through the pages to the end. And then he stilled and rubbed his forehead. 'You don't want any payment at all?'

She rubbed her hands up and down her arms. What kind of people was he used to dealing with? 'Of course I don't want any payment! I'm not entitled to any payment. Rightfully the land is yours. If you want to pay anyone a fee for leasing the land, then pay your mother.'

He sat back. 'I've offended you.'

Why did the wonder in his voice suddenly make her want to cry? Since Sarah's death, the silliest, most unexpected things could make her cry. 'You will if you keep going on in that vein.'

Her voice came out husky and choked. His gaze lowered to her mouth and it gave her a moment to study him. He had a strong jaw and lean lips and she couldn't tear her eyes away. She could keep telling herself that he wasn't sexy, but he was. His eyes darkened. A pulse throbbed in her bottom lip, swelling it and making it ache. The heat in the air between them sizzled with such unmistakable intensity it made her head whirl. With an oath, Cam pushed away from the table. He seized the teapot and started making tea. She closed her eyes. She'd been surrounded by death, preoccupied with it. Life wanted to reassert itself. This—her body's rebellion at her common-sense strictures—was normal.

The explanation didn't make the pounding in her blood lessen any, but it did start to clear the fog encasing her brain.

She jumped when Cam set a mug of tea in front of her, his face a mask. 'I'm sorry. I didn't mean to offend you. I'm just used to paying my own way.'

She wasn't. Not really. Her cold realisation dissipated the last of the heat. She'd always relied on staff or assistants to take care of her day-to-day needs. But she could learn. She *was* learning.

He hooked out his chair again and sat. 'A free ride feels wrong.'

'It's not a free ride. A free ride is if I also did the planting for you. You'd discussed that land with your mother. You had her permission to use it. Like you said, the fact it ended up on my lease agreement was simply an error or an oversight. Cameron, I have no plans for that land. I'm not losing out on anything.'

He didn't say anything.

'Besides, don't knock a free ride. I'm getting one—a dollar a week rent! Who'd have thought that was possible?'

His lips turned upwards, but it wasn't really a smile. 'You've brought two school-age children into the area. You're boosting the school's numbers and increasing its chances of remaining open. The town will think it a very good swap.'

Speaking of children… She rose and went to the window again to check on them. She laughed at what she saw. 'Are you sure they won't wear Boomer out?'

'I'm positive.' He eyed her as she took her seat again. 'They are safe with him. I promise.'

'Oh! Of course they are. I didn't mean…' She could feel herself starting to colour under his stare. The thing was, most days she felt as if she didn't know a darn thing about parenting at all. Maybe she did fuss a little too much, worry too much, but surely that was better than not fussing enough.

That was when the idea hit her.

He leant towards her, his eyes wary. 'What?'

She surveyed him over the rim of her mug. 'You're obviously not very comfortable with me just handing the land back to you.'

'You could make a tidy profit from the lease.'

'Believe me, the one thing I don't need to worry about is money.' Sarah had seen to that. 'But maybe,' she started slowly, allowing the idea to develop more fully in her mind, 'we could do a kind of swap. I'll give you the land…'

'In exchange for what?'

She rose and went to the window again. She loved those kids. Just how fiercely amazed her. She'd do anything for them. *Anything.* And what she needed to do most was provide them with a positive start here in Bellaroo Creek.

Cam stared at Tess as she peered out of the kitchen window again. She had a stillness and a straightness, even when agitated, that he found intriguing.

And she had the cutest little butt he'd ever seen. There'd probably been a hint of its perfect roundness in her tartan skirt yesterday if he'd been looking, but there was no hiding it in a pair of fitted jeans that hugged every curve with enviable snugness.

And today he was definitely looking!

For heaven's sake, he was male. Men looked at—and appreciated—the female form. It was how they were wired. It didn't mean anything.

But he hadn't looked at a woman in that way since Fiona, and—

With a scowl, he dragged his gaze away. He needed to keep on task. Tess was proposing a deal of sorts. He glanced up to find her watching him, her brow furrowed as if she couldn't figure him out. Not that he blamed her.

'You can take the contract and run,' she said. She walked back to the table, seized the contract, signed and dated it and then handed it back to him. 'Nothing more needs to be said. I don't believe you're beholden to me, not one jot.'

Honour kept him in his seat. Tess hadn't taken advantage of the situation as she could've done. As Lance and Fiona would've done. He did his best to clear the scowl from his face. She'd been reasonable and…generous. 'What kind of bargain were you going to propose, Tess?'

'I want to make moving to Bellaroo Creek a really positive experience for Ty and Krissie.'

She hadn't needed to say that out loud. He could see how much it meant to her. He wanted to tell her how much he admired her for it, but he didn't. He didn't want her to think he'd mean anything more by it than simple admiration. Because he wouldn't.

'But frankly I'm clueless.'

That snapped him back. 'About?'

She lifted her arms and let them drop. 'Everything! I didn't even know that was a lemon tree and yet you heard all our plans for it.'

Something inside him unhitched.

'I don't know the first thing about keeping chickens, but Krissie has her heart set on it. I expect I need a…a hutch or something.'

'Henhouse.'

'See? I don't even have the right vocabulary. And what about a vegetable garden? Other than supposing there's a lot of digging involved, I haven't the foggiest idea where to start.' She frowned. 'I expect I'll need compost.'

And, suddenly, Cam found himself laughing. 'Believe me, Tess, the one thing we aren't short of in Bellaroo Creek is compost.'

She gripped her hands on the table in front of her and leant towards him. 'Plus I need to get Ty a puppy, but is a puppy and chickens a seriously bad combination?'

'They don't have to be.' He leaned across and covered both of her hands with one of his own. She stiffened and he remembered the way he'd stiffened at her touch yesterday and was about to remove his hand when she relaxed. Her hands felt small and cold and instead of retreating he found his hand urging warmth into hers instead.

'So you want help building a henhouse and a veggie patch, and in selecting a dog?'

'It has to be a puppy. Apparently that's very important.'

Cam understood that. He nodded.

'And maybe some help choosing chickens?'

She winced as if she were asking too much, but it was all a piece of cake as far as he was concerned. 'Tess, helping you with that stuff is nothing more than being neighbourly.'

The townsfolk of Bellaroo Creek would have his hide if he didn't offer her that kind of support. Though—his lips twisted—he expected there'd be quite a few single farmers in the area who wouldn't mind offering her any kind of help whatsoever.

'Then…maybe we can agree to being good neighbours. That's something else I can learn to do.'

He frowned, but before he could say anything she leapt up to glance out of the window again. 'And until I manage to get one of my own, may I borrow your lawnmower?'

'Done.'

She swung around and beamed at him. 'Thank

you. Now watch me as I make a fresh pot of tea to make sure I'm doing it right.'

She had the kind of smile—when she really smiled—that could blow a man clean out of his boots. Mentally, he pulled his boots up harder and tighter.

'Why can't Cam come to our party?'

Excellent question. Tess glanced briefly in the rear-view mirror to give Krissie an encouraging smile. 'He said he had lots of work to do.'

'I bet he had to take time off work to bring Boomer around to play,' Ty said from the seat beside her. It was his turn in the front. 'His farm is really big, isn't it?'

'Six thousand hectares is what he said.' And Cameron didn't strike her as the bragging type. He was definitely the state-plain-facts type. 'Which I think is really, really big.'

'So he probably has loads and loads of work to do.'

Was that admiration or wistfulness in Ty's voice? She couldn't tell.

A mother would know.

She gulped. 'Good thinking, Ty, I expect you're right.'

His chest puffed out at her simple praise. Blinking hard, she concentrated on the road in front of her.

It only took three minutes to drive from their front door to the community hall in Bellaroo Creek's tiny main street. Across from the hall stood a row of late-Victorian townhouses—tall, straight, eye-catching, but with all their windows boarded up. Whatever businesses had operated from them were long gone. Once upon a time the town had been prosperous. Tess crossed her fingers. Hopefully they could help make the town prosperous again.

Unhooking her seat belt, she turned to the children. 'Ready?' They watched her so carefully. She knew they'd take their every cue from her. The realisation made her swallow. She had to get this just right.

Krissie leaned forward. 'Is this party really just for us?'

'It sure is, chickadee. Everyone is dying to meet us. They're so excited we've come to live in Bellaroo Creek.'

'What if they don't like us?' she whispered.

Tess feigned shock. 'Do you really think they won't like me?'

Krissie giggled. 'Not you, silly.'

'They'll love you,' Ty announced.

She knew what he was really saying was that he loved her and it made her heart swell and her eyes sting. 'And I absolutely promise that they'll love the two of you too.'

They stared at her with their identical brown eyes—eyes the same as Sarah's. They trusted her so much! She racked her brain to think of a way to make this easier for them.

'You know,' she started, 'it can be a bit awkward making new friends at first, and I bet they're just as worried that we should like them too.' She could see that thought hadn't occurred to either child. 'Sometimes it helps to have something ready to talk about. So…when you're talking to someone today you might like to ask them what their favourite thing about living in Bellaroo Creek is, or if they have a dog, or if they keep chickens.'

Both children's faces cleared immediately.

'Ooh!' She clapped her hands. 'I could send you both on a quest to find out what everyone thinks would be the best vegetables to grow in our backyard.'

Ty squinted up at her. 'Because that's important, right?'

'Vital,' she assured him.

He grinned. 'And you could find out how to make Cam's mum's cake.'

She pointed a finger at him. 'Excellent idea!' She straightened her shirt. 'And I'm going to remember to smile nicely at everyone and remember to say please and thank you in all the right places. Ready?'

The children nodded. They tumbled out of the car and, holding tight to each other's hands, they entered the hall together.

Tess blinked. There had to be at least thirty people in here! As well as one seriously long trestle table covered with more sandwiches, pies, quiches, cakes, slices and biscuits than Tess had seen altogether in one place. The sight of all that food, and all those faces, made her head spin. A hush fell over the crowd.

Thirty people, and yet for one craven moment she'd have given anything to swap ten of them for the familiar reassuring bulk of Cameron Manning. Which was crazy because she didn't know Cameron well enough for him to be either familiar or reassuring. But so far Bellaroo Creek consisted of their farmhouse, their lemon tree and Cameron.

All these people will become your community, your friends, too.

First-day nerves, that was all that this was. Taking a deep breath, Tess beamed about the room. 'Hi, I'm Tess, and this here is Ty and Krissie. We can't tell you how happy we are to be in Bellaroo Creek and how much we're looking forward to meeting everyone.'

A tall, straight woman detached herself from the crowd. 'I'm Lorraine Pritchard, and we're all absolutely delighted that you've joined our little community.'

And just like that the silence was replaced with a hubbub of voices, and the three of them were swept into the heart of the crowd. An older woman—Stacy Bennet, the schoolteacher—whisked Ty and Krissie off to join a small band of children, stopping by the refreshment table to make sure they armed themselves with a fairy cake each first, and thereby winning herself two friends for life.

'The children will be fine with Stacy,' Lorraine told her kindly.

Of course they would. The same way they'd been fine with Boomer this morning. It was just…she hated losing sight of them, even for a moment. Telling herself to stop being so silly, she turned back to Lorraine. The older woman took her arm. 'Come and meet everyone.'

It'd take her longer than a single afternoon to get everyone's names straight in her mind, but they were all so friendly and kind with their welcomes and their offers of assistance to help her settle in that in under ten minutes Tess felt wrapped in warmth. The glimmer of light that had taken up residence in her heart the moment her application had been accepted now became a fully floodlit arena.

She pressed her hands to her chest and blinked hard.

A group of women surrounded her. One handed her a mug of tea, another handed her a plate piled high with food. They filled her in on what produce was available from the general store and how to set up an account there. They shared their favourite online sites for ordering in school supplies, work boots and make-up. When she asked, they told her the date for the next CWA meeting and promised to meet her there.

Several men came up to her too. One to tell her he was her man if she ever decided to keep pigs. Another to let her know he could help her set up her own home brew if she wanted. Another introduced himself as the soccer coach for the Bellaroo Creek under tens team and told her that both Ty and Krissie were welcome when training started up in another month.

The entire town, it seemed, welcomed them with arms wide open and friendship in their hearts. Her earlier nerves suddenly seemed ludicrous.

'How are you doing, dear?' Lorraine said, coming up behind her. 'I hope we haven't overwhelmed you?'

'This is…' Tess swallowed and gestured around the room. 'It's just something else. I can't tell you how much I appreciate it.'

'Nonsense! We wanted to welcome you to town in style. Now may I introduce my future daughter-in-law, Fiona?'

'Lovely to meet you.' Tess balanced her mug on her plate and shook hands with the pretty young woman. They exchanged pleasantries for a couple of minutes before Fiona, with a glance back behind her, excused herself. Tess turned back to Lorraine. 'Thank you so much for the cake you left yesterday.

I can't tell you how much we appreciated it after that long drive.'

'You're welcome, my dear. I'm only sorry I couldn't be there to greet you in person.'

'That's okay, Cameron deputised honourably in your absence.'

Lorraine's head shot up. 'Cam?' Two beats went by then, 'Oh, I'm so glad to hear it.' Her hand fluttered to her throat. 'I've been meaning to ring him, but... Is he well?'

Tess thought about those broad shoulders and long legs and had to swallow. 'He seemed very well.'

Lorraine leaned forward, her eyes eager. 'Yes?'

She blinked. 'Umm... I mean, he obviously works hard, but he brought Boomer around to meet the children this morning, which was kind of him.'

'Oh!' Lorraine clapped her hands together, her eyes shining. 'Oh, I'm so pleased to hear that.'

She was? She continued to stare at Tess as if eager to hear any news about Cam that Tess was willing to share. Tess lifted a shoulder. 'There was a bit of a mix-up on the lease agreement, but we sorted it out.'

Lorraine stilled. 'Mix-up?'

'Something about forty hectares that belong to Cam, or that he was supposed to be leasing from you or something like that, accidentally being on the lease agreement I signed.'

Lorraine paled. 'Oh...no. Are you sure?'

Tess stilled then too because it was evident that

something was wrong. Very wrong. She wanted to ask what it was but manners prevented her. She rolled her shoulders. 'Perhaps I shouldn't have mentioned it.' She forced a wide smile, wanting to ease the other woman's evident anxiety. 'But I promise we sorted it out. He's happy with the outcome and so am I.'

A breath shuddered out of the older woman and she sent Tess a smile that signalled her relief. 'I'm very, *very* glad to hear that. If you see him, please give him my love.'

'Of course.' But…why didn't Lorraine give Cam her love in person?

Lorraine stared beyond Tess and suddenly straightened. 'Would you excuse me for a moment, Tess? I—'

Before she could move, however, a man Tess hadn't met charged up and kissed Lorraine's cheek, before turning to survey Tess. 'Would you introduce me to Bellaroo Creek's newest resident?'

Lorraine bit her lip. Finally she shook her head and said, 'Tess, this is my son, Lance.'

Cameron's brother? Tess hastily set her plate and mug on a nearby table and extended her hand. 'I'm very pleased to meet you.' He was prettier than Cameron with his blond good looks and golden tan, but neither his size nor his presence was anywhere near as commanding.

He grinned at her. He had one of those infectious

kinds of grins. 'Oh, ho! The single farmers in the district are sure going to be pleased to meet you.'

She laughed. And he had an easy charm his older brother totally lacked.

She'd met men like Lance before—full of fun, but often not much else. On closer inspection, though, the colour was high on his cheeks and she couldn't help feeling his joviality was forced.

'It's great to meet you, Tess. Welcome to Bellaroo Creek.'

'Thank you.'

'And as I'm not the kind of man to let the grass grow under my feet…'

Really? She didn't believe that for one moment.

'I'd like to talk business with you.'

The hair at her nape prickled. She folded her arms. 'Oh?'

'Lance.' Lorraine laid a hand on his arm. 'This is neither the time nor the place.'

He shook off his mother's touch. 'Of course it is.' He bounced on the balls of his feet, a fine sheen of perspiration filming his top lip and his forehead. 'Now I understand, Tess, that you have forty prime hectares on your allotment that are just going begging. I want to make you an offer you can't refuse.'

Several groups nearby stopped talking and turned to listen. Others moved forward.

'Oh, Lance, I can't believe this of you!' Lorraine hissed. 'I think—'

He held up a hand, his eyes glittering. 'I'd like to lease that land from you at very generous terms.'

Someone nearby snorted. Lance ignored it, but Lorraine's hand fluttered about her throat. 'Lance, please,' she whispered.

He rocked back on his heels. 'What do you say, Tess?'

That was when she realised thirty pairs of eyes watched her closely, waiting to see what she'd say, and instinct told her whatever she did or said now would seal her, Ty and Krissie's fate in Bellaroo Creek, for good or ill.

And she didn't know what would work for or against them.

She swallowed. She hadn't done anything wrong. All she could do was offer Lance the truth. 'I'm sorry, Lance, but I signed a contract this morning leasing that land to Cameron. I understood he had a right to it.'

Cameron was his brother. Surely Lance would be happy for him?

Lance stared at her, the blood draining from his face. 'But…I need that land more than he does. I *need* that canola contract.'

'Cam's spent the last two years improving that land,' somebody from the crowd said.

He had?

'Yeah, back off, Lance. Cam's earned the right to that land,' someone else called out.

Lance swung back to Tess, his face twisting and his eyes wild with panic. 'You've ruined me. You and Cam both.' His voice rose on each word. 'It's what he wants, and you've been party to that!' He stiffened. 'I hope you're happy?'

Happy? She was appalled!

One of the older farmers muttered, 'One can hardly blame Cam for that.' He lifted his voice. 'And it's sure as heck not Tess's fault. So like Stuart said, back off, Lance.'

Lance pointed a finger at her. Tess swallowed. She opened her mouth just as Ty came barrelling up, shaking, his small hands clenched to fists. 'Don't you yell at my auntie Tess!'

Bursting into tears, Krissie hurled herself at her aunt. Tess scooped her up and held her close, dangerously close to tears herself.

Fiona raced up and took Lance's arm. With an apologetic glance at Tess, she led him away.

Lorraine turned to her, pale, her hands shaking. 'Oh, Tess, I'm so sorry. I—'

Hauling Ty in close to her side, she said, 'Just give me a moment,' before leading the children to a quiet corner where she tried to quieten Krissie's sobs. Not easy when her insides were quivering and all she wanted to do was drop her head and cry too.

The luncheon had been so perfect. She'd started to feel like a part of the community. She'd thought everything was going to work out exactly as she needed it to. And then, bam!

Her head reeled. She found it hard to catch her breath. She closed her eyes and dragged air into her lungs. 'Shh, honey.' She rubbed Krissie's back. 'Everything is okay.'

It would be okay. She'd make sure it'd be okay. A setback, that was all this was.

'Why was that man angry?' Krissie hiccupped.

'It's not so much that he was angry as he was upset. He's very worried about some things.'

Her whole body shuddered. 'Is he going to hurt us?'

'No, honey, he's not.' She hugged Krissie close and then touched Ty's cheek. He was so quiet. 'I promise. Okay?'

''Kay,' he murmured.

'The man was being very silly and we don't need to worry about him at all.' She prayed they'd believe her, that they trusted her enough. Time for a brave face. 'You know what I need?' she whispered. 'A lamington. Are there any?'

'Ones with cream in them.'

'Ooh, yum.' She made her eyes wide. 'Let's go look.'

They each selected a lamington, they each took a bite, and then Tess caught Stacy's eye. 'Don't forget,' she whispered before the teacher reached them, 'I need the names of vegetables.'

They were laughing again by the time they reached the group of other children. Tess didn't doubt there'd be more questions tonight, but for now things were fine.

She moved back towards Lorraine and the group of women who surrounded her. 'Are the littlies okay?' one of the women asked her.

Tess hesitated, her gaze darting back to the circle of children. 'I think so.' She swallowed. She'd given an account of Ty and Krissie's circumstances in her application letter. Not a full account, perhaps, but full enough. She didn't doubt that everyone in the room knew about the death of their parents. 'It's just that they've been through so much in such a short space of time… Little things can unduly upset them.'

'An angry man isn't a little thing. Especially when you're five years old.'

Tess had to close her eyes for a moment. *An angry man*. The shaking started back up inside her. Lorraine touched her arm. 'I can't tell you how sorry I am, Tess. Lance has a lot on his mind at the moment, but that doesn't excuse his behaviour.'

Lorraine was obviously appalled.

'It wasn't your fault.' But… She twisted her hands together. 'Is there anything I ought to know?'

The women surrounding them discreetly melted away, leaving Tess and Lorraine alone. Lorraine gripped her hands together. 'Cameron and Lance have had the most dreadful falling out, Tess. They haven't spoken to each other in over ten months.'

Ten months!

Lorraine's eyes filled with tears. 'I...I certainly didn't expect any of that fallout to land in your lap, though. I'm absolutely mortified.'

The older woman's heartache tugged at her. But... 'That forty hectares?' she whispered.

Lorraine blinked hard and swallowed. 'I knew nothing about it, I promise.'

The shaking inside her started to slow.

'Tess, I can't tell you how sorry—'

She reached out to clasp the other woman's hands. 'There's no need to apologise further, Lorraine.' She had no desire to make things even harder for the other woman. Especially when she'd gone to so much trouble to welcome them to town so warmly. 'Let's forget about it.' She made herself smile and then turned to check on Ty and Krissie again. She prayed there hadn't been any permanent harm done there.

'Honey.' Lorraine moved in close so they were touching shoulders. 'I understand your concern. Your Ty and Krissie have had a lot to deal with, but...children are remarkably resilient, you know?'

She gave a shaky laugh. 'Are they?' She didn't have a clue.

'Yes, I promise. And I promise they'll be okay. All you can do is love them the best you can...as

you obviously do. All of us here in Bellaroo Creek
will do our best to become a second family to them.
It'll all work out in the end.'

The other women, who'd moved back in closer,
all nodded and murmured their agreement.

They made it sound so easy.

Why, then, was it proving so very, very hard?

CHAPTER THREE

CAM WENT TO knock on Tess's front door, but the sound of voices out the back had him redirecting his path around the side of the house.

Tess, Ty and Krissie all sat on a bright blue rug beside the lemon tree. They sat in a row—Tess in the middle—with legs stretched out in front of them and their backs to the sun, and him.

The scene hit him in a place he'd thought he'd locked up for good. For three beats of his heart a gnawing, ragged ache threatened to split him open. Reaching out, he steadied himself against the boards of the house. He'd dreamed of being part of a picture like this once. Ten short months ago, in fact, though it seemed like a lifetime ago now.

A family.

His jaw clenched. Lance and Fiona had stolen this from him.

A boulder of a lump stretched his throat. His temples pounded.

No! He refused to be beguiled by this dream

again. He would never again open himself up to the kind of betrayal Lance and Fiona had inflicted upon him.

Filling Kurrajong House with a family, that had all been a ludicrous, out-of-reach dream. He'd found that out the hard way, just like his father. Unlike his father, however, he had no intention of burying himself on Kurrajong Station and stewing in 'what might have beens' and regrets, and waiting for death to come claim him. He'd fill the gaps somehow.

He went to swing away, to retrace his steps to the privacy and solitude of Kurrajong where he could wipe this picture from his mind and replace it with his plans for Africa and adventure, but Ty chose that moment to look up at his aunt. In profile Cam recognised the little boy's frown and the way it changed his entire demeanour. Noted the hunching of his shoulders and the way he curled himself around his knees. Very slowly, Cam turned back.

'What if this isn't a good place?'

Tess tousled his hair, and, although he couldn't see her face, he knew detail for detail the smile she'd have sent the young boy. 'How can this not be a good place? Look, we have a lemon tree *and* sultana cake.' She gestured to the tree and then the plate that shared the blanket with them.

Ty's frown didn't abate. Tess's shoulders started to tighten.

'And what about all the nice people we met yesterday? Cam's mum, Mrs Pritchard, was lovely *and* she gave me her sultana cake recipe. Plus you guys were great and we now have the names for all the vegetables we should plant in our veggie garden. And what about Mrs Bennet? You both told me she's the nicest teacher in the world.'

'Yeah.' Ty grabbed a dandelion out of the lawn and shredded it.

'Suzie was nice,' Krissie volunteered, 'even if she thinks chickens are boring. She said we could come and play in her pool in the summer.'

'Nice.' Tess drew the word out, injecting it with what Cam supposed was the appropriate amount of enthusiasm.

'Mikey and Ryan have dogs,' Ty said, but there wasn't a fleck of enthusiasm in his voice.

Cam shifted his weight. What the hell…?

'What if bad men keep yelling at us?' Krissie blurted out.

'Chickadee, that man yesterday wasn't bad.' She gave Krissie a one-armed hug. 'Like I said before, he was upset, that's all. And remember, people yell for lots of different reasons.'

'You don't yell,' Ty said.

'Believe me, if I saw one of Cam's sheep in my veggie patch, I'd be yelling my head off!'

Neither child laughed.

'But that man yelled at you!' Ty burst out.

Someone had yelled at Tess? Cam stiffened. He stepped into the yard. 'Howdy, gang.'

Both children immediately swung around, fear frozen on their faces. Cold, hard anger lanced through him because then he knew—someone had hurt these kids, had frightened them, and he wanted to find out who it was and tear them from limb to limb.

'Hey, Cam, nice to see you.'

Behind the children's backs, Tess mouthed, *Smile* at him, and it suddenly hit him how intimidating he must appear to these two small kids.

He forced his face to relax into a kind of half grin, although his blood burned and the surface of his skin prickled. 'You guys have the nicest spot in the sun. Mind if I join you?'

'We'd like that.' Tess shuffled over. Both children remained glued to her side. 'Want some sultana cake?'

He glanced at the plate, hunger rumbled through him, but he shook his head.

'Did you bring Boomer?' Ty asked.

Cam kicked himself for not bringing the dog. 'Sorry, mate, I didn't. I left Boomer in charge of the sheep.'

'That is one smart dog,' Tess said, and Cam watched as the worst of the fear and shadows slowly drained from Ty's and Krissie's faces.

'I just dropped by to talk lawnmowers. I have a

ride-on and thought I might whizz it around this place tomorrow if that suited you.'

Tess shook her head, her hair so dark and her skin so golden it made him ache in familiar and unfamiliar ways. 'Oh, no, you don't, Cameron Manning. I can mow my own lawn, thank you very much. Though, a lesson in how to operate your ride-on would be greatly appreciated.'

It was obviously important to her to do it herself. He bit down on his urge to argue with her, although it chafed at him. He nodded. 'Right.'

'Woo hoo!' She punched the air. 'I get to use a ride-on mower. How much fun will that be?'

Krissie finally smiled.

'So how did yesterday's luncheon go?' He rested back on his hands, deliberately casual.

'Ooh.' Tess rubbed her hands together. 'There must've been thirty people there.'

'It was a Saturday. Everyone would've made an effort.'

Ty scowled. 'You didn't.'

'No,' he agreed. 'But I really wish I had.' And he meant it.

His stomach suddenly rolled. Why hadn't he gone? Eleven months ago he'd have been there. But since Lance and Fiona... Nausea burned his throat. Despite all his precautions he was turning into a recluse like his father.

No! He snapped the thought off. He was leaving Bellaroo Creek so he *didn't* turn into his father. He'd forge a new life for himself—an involved and engaging life. The kind of life he couldn't have in Bellaroo Creek.

Still… The idea of socialising had become anathema and he'd buried himself in station work, rarely going into town. None of that changed the fact that he wished he'd attended yesterday's luncheon.

Who had yelled at Tess and spooked the kids?

'A bad man yelled at Auntie Tess,' Krissie confided.

'Who?'

Ty scowled again. 'His name was Lance and we don't know if we want to live here any more.'

Lance?

He flicked a glance at Tess and a hand reached inside his chest to wring his heart. The raw grief in her eyes as she surveyed the children made his jaw ache. She glanced up, caught his gaze and tried to smile, but he saw the effort it cost her. That was when he realised she couldn't speak for the tears blocking her throat, and he sensed that crying in front of the children was the last thing she wanted. And probably the last thing either Ty or Krissie needed.

'Oh, Lance!' he pshawed. 'You don't have to worry about Lance.'

Krissie bit her lip. 'He's not a bad man?'

He was a black-hearted traitor, but Cam had enough justice in him still to know Lance would be horrified to find he'd become a bogey man to these kids. 'Nah, he's all hot air, you know? He makes a lot of noise, but he wouldn't hurt a fly. I should know, because he's my little brother.'

Relief rushed into both the children's faces and it hit him then how much these kids trusted him. He didn't know how or why—whether it was a carry-over from all of Tess's positivity when they'd arrived on Friday, or because he'd brought Boomer over to play, or the fact he knew Old Nelson the blue-tongue lizard, but it made his chest cramp. He couldn't let these kids rely on him too much. He was their neighbour, nothing more. But instinct told him he'd need to tread carefully—these kids needed kid-glove handling.

He ached to quiz them more about Lance—why he had yelled at Tess—but the kids needed to take their minds off yesterday's incident. They needed to remember the good things about living in Bella-roo Creek. They needed to be allowed to get on with their fresh start without fear and setbacks.

'Now I don't know if this will be agreeable to you guys or not, but because I worked so hard yesterday, and because Boomer's taking care of things today, I get to take the rest of today off.' He rubbed his chin and pursed his lips as if in a pretence of thought. 'So I was thinking you might like to go and check out some chickens and puppies.'

All three faces on the blanket before him lit up.

He immediately tried to temper their enthusiasm. 'Today we only look because these things take a lot of careful thought and planning. It's a big responsibility to own an animal and you need to be very sure that the choice you make is the right one for you, you understand?'

All three heads nodded in unison. It struck him how young Tess was—she couldn't be much older than twenty-five. Too young for taking on all the responsibility she had.

Ty jumped up. 'Can we leave right now?'

He suppressed a grin at the young boy's eagerness. 'You'll need time to get ready. I'll pick you up in an hour. Promise you'll be ready?'

'Yes!' Both children raced indoors and Tess laughed. She actually laughed as she watched them and it lightened the unexplained weight that had settled across his shoulders. To see pleasure in her face instead of fear and grief...

She leapt to her feet. He rose more slowly, finding it suddenly difficult to catch his breath. She grabbed his arm, reached up on tiptoe and kissed his cheek. 'I could kiss you, Cameron! Thank you.'

He went to point out that she'd done exactly that, but he couldn't push a single sound out of his throat. He went to tell her to call him Cam, but his full name sounded so bewitching on those charming lips of hers, he found himself saying nothing at all.

And then she hugged him—hard and fierce—

and it knocked the sense and the breath clean out of his body. Every sweet curve Tess possessed pressed against him, and his body soaked up her warmth and vigour. It brought him to aching life and sent a surge of primitive hunger racing through him with the swiftness of a rabbit startled in the undergrowth. A wildfire licked along his veins…carrying the same danger that fire did out here in the bush.

Reason screamed at him to move away. Instead, one of his arms snaked around her waist and he pulled her in closer, hugged her back. His hand rested against the top of her hip. He wanted to move his hand lower, he wanted to mould her against him, wanted her soft and pliant and…

He felt rather than heard her quick intake of breath. She stiffened. A heartbeat passed. A heartbeat in which the fire raging through him threatened all of his control, and then she softened against him.

He let his hand drift down to cup her bottom and lift it against him. She arched into him. He groaned. He couldn't help it.

Her hands drifted down his chest, her face lifted to his, her eyes soft and her lips parted.

He wanted to taste her. He wanted to explore the fullness of her bottom lip and—

For God's sake, she hugged you out of gratitude. She wasn't inviting you to maul her like some low-life sleaze!

He recalled the raw pain he'd witnessed in her

eyes a moment before and, rather than snap away, he eased her out of his arms gently. 'Sorry, Tess.' His voice came out raspy and hoarse. 'I forgot myself for a moment.'

She blinked twice before the mistiness cleared from her eyes. Her cheeks flushed bright red. 'Oh! I—' She swung away. 'You and me both. I'm sorry. It's been an emotional morning.'

He shrugged and tried to appear as casual for her as he had for the children earlier. 'No harm done.'

She turned back to him. 'No harm done,' she echoed, her eyes searching his to test that truth. They both stood there awkwardly until she glanced at her watch. 'So you'll be back at around eleven?'

He snapped to and nodded.

'Should I pack a picnic?' She smiled impishly and everything slowly returned to normal—the colour of the sky, the sound of birdsong, the racing of his pulse. 'You wouldn't believe how much food there was at yesterday's do. And somehow most of the leftovers ended up in my car.'

He stared at her lips—they were more plum than rose. Hunger stretched through him as he took in the fullness of her bottom lip. His pulse began to race again. 'Sounds great,' he said, backing up. 'I'll see you in a while.'

He shot around the house and back towards his homestead. It occurred to him that burying himself out on his station for the last ten months might not have been the wisest course of action after all.

Cam's four-wheel-drive pulled up out the front and Tess hauled in a deep breath and locked the front door. Ty and Krissie raced towards the car with all the alacrity of children promised their heart's desire.

Cam had done that. He'd found the perfect way to remind them of all the exciting potential that living in Bellaroo Creek could bring. They'd gone from the doldrums to delight.

But she should never have kissed him. She most certainly shouldn't have hugged him.

And yet, even now, her body throbbed with a primitive hunger. She yearned to explore each and every line of his powerful body—naked. She craved his hands on her again—gentle hands, knowing hands. Oh, so knowing. Her knees quivered before she could stop them.

Enough of that!

She kicked herself into action and moved down the path, sidestepping Old Nelson who currently sunned himself on the cement path. Cam met her at the gate to take the picnic basket from her. He searched her face. She let him—freely and openly. She searched his face too. It was amazing how much information they could convey to each other without a word. He liked how she looked, and he wanted her in the same way she wanted him, but...

They both sighed and nodded at the same moment. Romance wasn't on the cards for either of them. She didn't know his reasons, but she knew her own. She'd been selfish her entire life—selfish and clueless—but not any more.

I won't let you down again, Sarah. I promise.

'Where are we going?' Krissie demanded the minute Cam started the car and eased it onto the road.

'Our first stop is the O'Connell farm. Blue O'Connell has the best layers in the entire district. He has show chickens too. He takes out the blue ribbon every year at the Parkes agricultural show. What's more, his black lab has had a litter of puppies.'

Ty started talking so fast Tess couldn't understand a word he said.

'Steady, buddy.' Cam laughed. 'We've also a litter of border collie pups—like Boomer—to check out as well as some poodles.'

When they reached the farm, the children literally launched themselves out of the car. They both jumped and danced—at least in Krissie's case—and jumped and hopped—in Ty's—with uncontained excitement. Tess watched them and something inside her swelled. To see their faces alive with hope instead of fear, to see them grinning at the unknown farmer who came to greet them rather than backing up towards her with suspicion clouding their eyes, lifted something inside her.

To see them, for just one moment, truly happy. It made her want to weep. It made her hope. It made her think that coming to Bellaroo Creek had been the perfect plan after all.

'Are you Mr O'Connell?' Krissie asked.

'That I am, little miss.'

'I'm Krissie.' She walked right up to the farmer and held her hand out. 'And we're here to see your chickens.'

Sweet Lord, she must want a chicken badly.

Ty hung back for all of five seconds before bursting forward as well. 'And your puppies too.'

'Well, young folk, that's something I can certainly accommodate. Come right this way.' With a wink and a smile for Tess and Cam, he led the children towards the barn.

'Are you okay?' Cam asked, those green eyes of his seeming to plumb her soul.

'Oh!' She pressed both hands to her chest. 'Oh, Cameron, I think they're going to be fine after all.'

He tipped his hat back—a dusty, sweat-stained Akubra. 'Why wouldn't they be?'

She had to swallow before she could speak. 'The last three months have been just awful. And…'

'And?'

Beneath her hand her heart pounded. 'I didn't know if they would ever be happy again,' she whispered. 'I didn't know if I could help them be happy again, but… But your mum was right. Children are resilient.' This was the beginning of the brand-new start she'd been hoping for. Now she just had to focus on keeping them all on an even keel and making sure they felt secure.

'C'mon.' He took her arm. 'I have a feeling you need this as much as they do.'

They found Krissie sitting in a pen with the silliest piece of feathered nonsense that Tess had ever seen perched on her lap. It looked as if it should be worn on some posh hat for Melbourne's Spring Carnival. Krissie raised her big brown eyes. 'This one,' she whispered, hope so alive in her face it stole Tess's breath.

Cam stiffened and opened his mouth. Tess dug her elbow in his ribs. 'Can't you see it's true love?' she murmured, leading him further into the depths of the barn.

'But it's a show chicken. It won't lay a tuppence worth of eggs.'

'And yet Krissie doesn't care…and neither do I.' She wanted to sing! 'Let's find Ty.'

They found him being licked to within an inch of his life by six puppies. Cute, round, roly-poly puppies. When he saw Tess and Cam he picked one of the puppies up and clambered to his feet. He hitched up his chin. 'I thought about it very long and hard,' he vowed. 'This is the absolutest, bestest puppy in the world for me. I don't need to look any more.'

Cam's mouth dropped open. 'We were only supposed to look!'

But she'd started laughing. 'Cameron, you have a lot to learn about children if you really thought all we were ever going to do today was just look.'

They went home with a chicken and a wire cage loaned to them by Mr O'Connell, a puppy, a dog basket, a collar and lead, and plenty of pet food.

And their picnic.

Tess set up a card table in the backyard to keep the food out of reach of their furred and feathered friends, and two camp chairs for her and Cam. Children and animals cheerfully settled on the blanket until they'd finished eating, and then Krissie and Ty set about introducing Fluffy and Barney to the backyard.

Tess selected a pikelet liberally slathered in butter and jam and bit into it, closing her eyes for a moment to savour it. If she didn't stop eating like this soon, she'd outgrow all her clothes. She took a second bite. 'I can't believe that chicken is following Krissie about as if it's a dog.'

'I can't believe you bought a White Bearded Silky instead of a Leghorn or a Rhode Island or…or anything that's a proven layer. You know that thing is going to lay next to no eggs.'

She just grinned at him. 'Have a piece of sultana cake.'

He had a piece of fruitcake instead. 'And a black Labrador?' He shook his head.

'Labrador puppies are the cutest in the world.'

'They don't stop being stupid until they're about four years old. It'll chew everything it can find, you know?'

'That'll teach the kids to pick up after themselves. And while Barney may not prove to be the cleverest of dogs, I suspect he's going to be loving and loyal.'

'He'll never be a working dog.'

'We don't need a working dog.' She polished off her pikelet and licked her fingers. 'Cameron, I know we're breaking every rule of being proper country folk, but look how happy they are.' She found herself grinning like an idiot. 'How can that be a bad thing?'

He glanced at her and those green eyes of his softened. 'It's not, I guess. Not when you put it like that. I just can't help feeling you've taken on more work than you realise. And I'm responsible for that. If I'd known earlier what would happen—'

'I'm glad you didn't! You're responsible for the kids remembering all the good things they wanted from our move to Bellaroo Creek. You're responsible for them being happy that we moved here rather than afraid. Do you always focus on the negatives rather than the positives?'

He didn't answer. His eyes had lowered to her mouth and there was absolutely nothing negative about his gaze. What if he had kissed her earlier?

What would that have been like? She swallowed. Heat circled in slow spirals through her veins. She recalled in microscopic detail the feeling of being pulled up hard against him and the need that had roared through her.

The world contracted about them. She touched her lips—lips sensitised beyond measure. Her index finger traced her bottom lip. It swelled and throbbed... until she encountered something sticky.

Sticky? She closed her eyes in sudden mortification. Jam!

She had jam all over her face? No wonder Cameron was staring. She scrubbed it off and when she opened her eyes she found him staring straight out in front of him at his precious forty hectares.

She scowled but it didn't slow the thud of her heartbeat.

'Why did Lance yell at you?'

She shifted on her chair. Lorraine had said Cameron and Lance hadn't spoken in ten months. She didn't want to make that situation worse.

'I will find out so you might as well tell me.'

She slumped on a sigh. 'Fine, but I'll only tell you if you fill me in on what's going down with the two of you.'

His nose curled. It shouldn't look sexy. *It didn't look sexy!* 'I'm surprised nobody filled you in about it yesterday. It's no secret.'

His curled lip told her that while it might not be

a secret, he didn't enjoy talking about it. She pulled in a breath. 'Whatever it is, it's certainly upsetting your mother.'

He snorted. She didn't understand that.

'Ten months ago,' he clipped out, 'I was engaged to Fiona.'

She stared. Did he mean the same Fiona who… 'Tall, blonde, ponytail?'

'That's the one.'

She stiffened. 'Oh!'

He smiled but there was no warmth in it. 'Exactly.'

They both stared out at the backyard, silent for the moment. 'I, umm…take it,' she started, 'that you and Fiona hadn't broken up before she and Lance…'

'You take it right.'

Ouch!

She opened her mouth to say something, anything that would offer comfort or commiseration, but he glared at her and shook his head. 'Don't.'

Right. She closed her mouth again.

They were both quiet for a long time. Eventually she moistened her lips. 'Lance wanted to lease the forty hectares from me. When I told him I'd already signed the lease over to you he…became a little upset.'

His eyes narrowed, but he still didn't look at her. 'He wanted to lease that land?'

'Uh-huh.'

His nostrils flared. 'I knew he was behind that.'

Um… 'I'm pretty positive your mother had no part in it, though.'

That made him swing to her. 'Oh, really?' His scorn could blast the skin from a person's frame. She darted a glance towards the children. He swore softly. 'Sorry.'

He raked a hand back through his hair. 'Look, I'm still angry that I didn't see it coming, that I didn't see what was happening right under my nose. That he was—'

He broke off. 'I underestimated him. None of that is your fault, though.'

'I'd have said believing in your family was a good thing, not a bad one.'

He didn't reply. She pulled in a breath. 'Look, yesterday your mother seemed appalled and shocked when I told her about the mix-up with the forty hectares. I doubt very much she feigned that.' She bit her lip and then shrugged. 'I liked her.'

His lips twisted. 'And let me guess, despite my brother's bad behaviour you like him too?'

She thought about that for a moment. 'Hmm, no, I'm not convinced I do. I don't much like being yelled at. He owes me an apology and until I receive one he's a…' He'd stolen Cam's fiancée! She tilted her chin. 'He's a weaselling, snivelling, black-hearted swine.'

Cam stared at her, his jaw slack, and then he

threw his head back and laughed. The sound rippled through her, warming her all over. Both Ty and Krissie glanced across at them and grinned. It made Tess realise what little laughter they'd had in their lives these last few months. And probably quite a while before then too if the truth be told.

Oh, Sarah.

At the thought of her beautiful dead sister any desire to laugh along with Cam fled. 'Cam, about your mum...'

His face shuttered closed. 'She's made it clear where her loyalties lie.'

'She loves you!' She couldn't keep the shock out of her voice.

'Then she has a funny way of showing it. Besides—' he rounded on her '—this is none of your business.'

'You should talk to her.'

He didn't say anything. She clenched and unclenched her hands. Lorraine's loyalties were obviously torn—she didn't want to lose either son. Tess understood that, but...

She leaned across and touched his arm. 'I'm serious, Cameron. I think you need to speak to her. I think the farm is in trouble. Big trouble. I think she needs you.'

The same way Sarah had needed her. Only, Tess had let her down and now she had to live with that knowledge for the rest of her life.

'Trouble? What makes you think that?'

She didn't want Cam making the same mistakes she had. 'Lance said he needed that canola contract. He implied the farm was in danger.' She bit her lip. 'He thinks you want to ruin him.'

Cam shook his head. 'I don't much care what Lance thinks any more.'

She understood that, but…

He turned to her. 'Look, Tess, the problems associated with my mother and Lance's station is none of my concern any more. Lance has made that clear through his actions and my mother has made it clear by virtue of her silence.'

She chafed her arms against a sudden chill. Three months ago she'd lost her sister. She'd do anything—*anything*—to have Sarah back for just one hour. And yet Cam was willing to turn his back on the only family he had? Lance might be a lost cause, but couldn't Cam see how much his mother loved him?

He rose. 'I'll bring the mower around tomorrow.'

'Thank you.'

He called out a goodbye to the kids and disappeared around the side of the house. Tess rose to find a cardigan and snuggled into it until she started to feel warm again.

CHAPTER FOUR

CAM CLEANED THE last of the tack. He glanced at the neatly aligned rows of bridles and lead ropes, and at the newly polished saddles, but two hours' worth of rubbing and buffing hadn't helped ease the itch between his shoulder blades.

With a frown, and a muffled curse that had no direct object, he strode out of the tack room and into the machinery shed to leap on a trail bike and kick it into life. He pointed it in the direction of the northern boundary fence and let loose with the throttle, even though he knew Fraser had trawled along that boundary through the week to check the fences.

He belted along the track for ten minutes when, with another muffled curse, he turned the bike back in the direction of the homestead. Dumping the bike back in the machinery shed, he grabbed several assorted lengths of wood and a roll of chicken wire and threw them, along with his toolbox, into the back of one of the station's utes and, with a final muffled curse, headed next door to Tess's.

He might be planning to sever his ties with Bella-roo Creek, but he couldn't leave a lone woman with two dependent kids to flounder on her own. Not on land he was ultimately responsible for. Not when it was his fault she now had a puppy and a chicken to look after on top of everything else.

Talk to her. That was what Tess had said about his mother.

He swiped a hand through the air. His mother would always have a home with him. She knew that, even if she chose to never accept it.

I think the farm is in trouble.

That was none of his business any more. He fish-tailed the ute to a halt in front of Tess's cottage and the itch between his shoulder blades intensified. He stared out of the windscreen and shook his head. The thought uppermost in his mind, it seemed, wasn't on building a chicken coop or wondering why his mother refused to come out to Kurrajong, but what Tess might be wearing today—jeans or a skirt?

He rubbed his eyes. When he lowered his hand it was to find Ty and Barney barrelling down the side of the house towards him. 'Hey, Cam!'

He pushed his door open and found a grin. 'Hey, Ty, how's Barney settling in?'

'I love him best of all dogs in the world!'

It struck him then that Ty looked just like any other seven-year-old boy who'd just got his first puppy—carefree, excited, his face shadow-free.

'He's a mighty fine-looking puppy,' Cam agreed, realising he'd helped to make those shadows retreat. The knowledge awed him, humbled him. He reached behind him to scratch his back.

Then Tess came tripping around the side of the house and all rational thought stopped for more beats of his pulse than he had the wit to count. Shorts. Tess wore a pair of scarlet-coloured shorts and a pale cream vest top. Her bare arms, bare legs and shoulders all gleamed in the autumn sunlight. She made him think of fields of ripening wheat, of cream and honey and nutmeg, of spiced apples and camping under the stars. She made him think of his mother's sultana cake—his favourite food in the world. He curled his fingers against his palms to stop from doing something daft and reaching out to stroke a finger down her arm.

'Hello, Cameron.'

He swallowed and then simply nodded, unsure if his voice would work.

'Auntie Tess said Barney did really good for a puppy. We've only had one accident.'

Cam winced. 'I, uh…'

Her eyes danced. 'Apologise again and I'll thump you. That puppy has been a source of pure joy.' She glanced at his ute and then planted her hands on her hips and sent him a mock glare. 'Where's my lawnmower?'

He grimaced. 'My station manager is currently lying beneath it trying to fix a fuel leak.'

'Ouch.'

'It should be fixed in the next day or so.' He didn't want her using it if it wasn't a hundred per cent safe.

She gestured with her head and turned. 'Come and join the party.'

He followed her. He didn't even try to keep from ogling the length of her legs or taking an inventory of the innate grace with which she moved. She was like some wonderful and exotic creature who'd deigned to live among the mundane and the humdrum. A creature whose beauty took one out of the mundane and humdrum for a few precious moments.

He wondered what she'd done for a living before she'd moved to Bellaroo Creek—maybe she'd been a dancer. He opened his mouth to ask, but they'd rounded the house and Krissie sat on a blanket with that darn chicken on her lap and when she glanced up and saw him she sent him a grin of such epic proportions it cracked his chest wide open.

He had to swallow before he could speak. 'Did Fluffy have a good night?'

'She slept in her cage in the laundry, but I think she'd be happier sleeping in my bedroom.'

Tess sent him a bare-teethed grimace that almost made him laugh. One could toilet train a puppy, but a chicken...? 'Well, honey, I've come around to build Fluffy her very own house.'

Krissie's bottom lip wobbled. 'Barney slept in Ty's room.'

He crouched down beside her. 'The thing is, Krissie, chickens aren't like puppies or kittens. They like the fresh air and they like to see the stars at night and be able to come and go as much as they please. So, as much as Fluffy loves you, she'll be happier out here in the yard.'

She stared at him and he held his breath. 'She'll get her very own house, right?'

'That's right.'

'A nice one?'

'One that she'll love,' he promised.

Her face cleared. 'I can show you a picture of Fluffy's dream house!' She plonked Fluffy down on the grass and raced inside.

'Oh, good Lord.' Tess groaned. 'I have no idea what she has in mind, Cameron.'

He had sudden visions of a hot-pink Barbie house and gulped. And then he glanced around. A collection of plastic planters in assorted shapes and sizes battled for space from the back of the house to the lemon tree. 'Where on earth did all these seedlings come from?'

Tess planted her hands on her hips. Sweet hips... long, lovely legs...pretty arms. Cam curled his fingers into his palms again. With a silent curse he uncurled them and shoved them into his pockets. Deep into his pockets.

'Everyone has been so kind. At Saturday's luncheon Ty, Krissie and I mentioned we'd like to start our own veggie garden and asked for advice on what vegetables we should grow.'

He shook his head, but he couldn't help grinning. 'I guess you got your answer.'

She grinned back. 'I guess we did.'

Her plum-coloured lips gleamed temptingly in the sunlight. His heart thumped. He kept his hands firmly in his pockets. The itch started up again with a vengeance.

Krissie reappeared brandishing a magazine. 'This one!' She held it up for them to see.

'That's an awful lot of house for one chicken, Krissie,' Tess said.

Krissie's bottom lip wobbled. 'But we'll get more chickens, remember? Fluffy will need friends for when I'm at school.'

She turned liquid eyes to Cam and they melted him on the spot. He rolled his shoulders, risked removing his hands from his pockets to take the magazine and survey the picture more fully. 'Oh, I think we can manage something like this.' He frantically recalculated the amount of wood in his ute with the amount he still had at the homestead.

'Give me a list of what we need and I'll go into the stock and station store to get supplies,' Tess said, as if reading his mind.

It wouldn't be cheap. He grimaced. He should've

found a way to talk Krissie into something less grand and—

'We're good for it, Cameron. It isn't a problem,' Tess said, again as if reading his mind, which unsettled him. He normally maintained a quiet reserve that made him hard to read. It had been one of the things Fiona had complained about. But this woman, it seemed, had only to glance at him to know what he was thinking.

But her plump dusky lips curved up with such promise he found he didn't mind at all…or, at least, not as much as he suspected he should.

'Can I help you build it?' Ty breathed, his eyes alight.

'I'll definitely need a helper—a foreman. It's a big job, Ty, and I'll need your help.'

Ty's eyes grew as big as cabbages, his chest puffed out. That awe hit Cam again as he pulled his cell phone from his pocket. Surveying Krissie's dream chicken coop, and doing his best to keep his eyes from the plump temptation of Tess's lips, he placed an order at the stock and station store.

They spent the afternoon on Phase One of the chicken coop. Tess couldn't believe Cam's patience with Ty or the way her nephew blossomed under his quiet but authoritative guidance. He'd lacked a male role model for so long.

Eventually, though, both children wandered off to

check on Old Nelson. And then Ty set about teaching Barney how to play fetch while Krissie fell asleep on the blanket beneath the shade of the lemon tree, leaving Fluffy free to scratch about the yard.

Tess glanced at Cam whistling idly as he nailed boards to the frame he'd built. Something inside her shifted. Ever since that moment yesterday when she'd hugged him, she'd grown increasingly aware of the breadth of his shoulders, of the flex and play of the muscles in his arms, and of the fresh-cut-grass scent that followed in his wake and stirred something to life inside her. Something she desperately tried to ignore.

The sun shone brightly, but not too fiercely, picking out the lighter highlights in his chestnut hair. Fiona had thrown this man over for Lance? Tess snorted. What a loser! The woman quite obviously had her head screwed on backwards. Lance might dazzle with those playboy good looks of his, but when a woman looked at Cam she was left in no doubt that he was all man.

One hundred per cent fit and honed man.

And the longer Tess stared at him, the more that thing inside her stirred and fluttered and stretched itself into heart-beating, mouth-drying sentience.

Thoughts of Lance, though, slid an unwelcome reminder through her. The expression on Lorraine's face—that mixture of anxiety, regret and heartbreak—rose in her mind and she bit back a sigh.

'You want to tell me what's on your mind?'

She blinked, and then realised Cam had caught her out blatantly staring at him. The skin on her face and neck burned. 'Oh…I…nothing.'

'Why don't I believe you?'

He wielded a hammer as if he'd been born to it. She dragged her gaze from muscled forearms lightly dusted with hair, and the pull of lean brown hands. She tried desperately to dispel thoughts of what else those hands might be expert at.

She clenched her eyes shut and counted to five. For pity's sake! She didn't need this at the moment— this wild, desperate ache. She needed to remain focused on the children. On not letting Sarah down. On making amends.

'Tess?'

She went back to tacking chicken wire to the frame of their mansion of a chicken house, the way he'd shown her, but she couldn't resist another glance at him. The brilliance of his eyes struck her afresh. She swallowed and shrugged. 'Oh, I was just thinking about stuff you'd no doubt declare me nosy for contemplating.'

He set his hammer down. 'Like?'

Keep your mouth shut. She set her hammer down too. 'Like how a man who is as gentle with children and animals as you could just ignore that his mother might be in trouble.'

He stiffened as if she'd slapped him.

'I said it was nosy,' she muttered, though she wasn't certain she was actually apologising.

'You're not wrong there.'

Minding her business was the wisest course of action. She knew that. Cam was a grown-up. He knew what he was doing. She swallowed. She used to be really good at minding her own business.

'You must really hate Lance if you haven't spoken to him in ten months.' She shivered. She understood his bitterness. She really did, but… 'How can you stand to live in the same town as him when you bear that much resentment?'

He eyed her for an interminable moment. It made her chest constrict. 'I'm not planning on staying for that much longer, Tess.'

He hammered in a nail with more force than necessary, and a sickening thump started up in her stomach. 'What?'

He set his hammer back down and glared at her. 'In two months I'll be out of this godforsaken town and Lance can sink or swim under his own steam. I've washed my hands of him and his tantrums and his so-called troubles.'

'But…' Cameron couldn't leave!

'What about your mother?' she burst out.

He picked the hammer up again. 'I expect my leaving will be a blessing for her. With me gone, tensions will ease.' He hammered in another nail.

'Besides, like I told you, my mother has made it clear where her loyalties lie.'

Tess's mouth opened and closed. 'Can't you see her loyalties are being torn?'

'By remaining in the same house as Lance and Fiona she's given them her tacit approval.'

'You mother is not the type of woman who would ever kick her offspring out of her house, regardless of what they've done.' She planted her hands on her hips. 'But that doesn't mean she doesn't love you.' Couldn't he see that? 'Do you really mean to make her choose between the two of you? She's not responsible for the things Lance has done.'

'My leaving means she won't have to choose.'

She glanced at Krissie and an ache exploded in her chest. Cam's anger and bitterness were warping him and tearing him apart. Couldn't he see that? 'Oh, Cameron, it's been ten months.'

He strode around and seized her chin, his eyes blazing. 'And you naively think that time can heal all wounds?'

His fingers were gentle but his voice was hard. He smelled of wood and grass and sweat.

He paused and she swallowed, aching at the pain she sensed behind the flint of his eyes.

He scanned her face and then released her with a shake of his head. 'Why does this matter so much to you?'

She had to take a step away from him. He was

too…much. Too much for her senses. Too much for her hormones. And the hardness in him clashed too deeply with the places that grieved inside her. 'I just lost my sister, Cam. I never appreciated her enough. I wish I had but I didn't. And now I've lost her and I can't get her back.'

He paled.

'I have no one now but Ty and Krissie. Don't get me wrong, they make up for everything, but…you have a mother who loves you and I'm jealous.' She tried to smile. He had a brother too, but she left that unsaid. In his shoes, would she be able to forgive Lance?

His eyes darkened, his hand half lifted as if to touch her cheek…and then he wheeled away.

She hunched her shoulders, wishing she hadn't started this conversation. Wishing she'd left well alone. She tried to make her voice bright. 'Where will you go when you leave Bellaroo Creek?'

He turned back. 'Africa. I'm an advisor for a charity whose mission is to increase agricultural production in Third World countries. I've requested a field position.'

'Wow!' She stared at him. 'Just…wow! That's amazing.' She swallowed and chafed her arms. 'What an adventure.'

'I'm hoping so.'

'Is it a secret?'

'I haven't told anyone, if that's what you mean.' He shifted his weight to plant his legs firmly.

She tried another smile and mimicked zipping her mouth shut to let him know she wouldn't say anything to anyone, and she had a feeling he had to fight back a smile of his own. She'd like to make him smile for real. 'We'll miss you, Cameron. You've been just about the best neighbour we city slickers could've had.'

His eyes widened. He blinked and then they narrowed. It made her want to fidget. Did he think she was making some kind of a move on him? Her spine stiffened and her chin shot up. 'You can lose that nasty suspicion right now,' she shot at him. 'Even if I was in the market for something more, I'm not stupid enough to get involved with a man on the rebound.' She folded her arms. 'In fact, I'm starting to think the sooner you leave, the better!'

He grinned then—a true-blue, solid-gold grin that hooked up his mouth and made his eyes dance. For a moment all Tess could make out was the brightness of the sun, the sound of the breeze playing through the leaves of the lemon tree and the force of that smile. She blinked and the rest of the world slowly surged back into focus.

'From where I'm standing, Tess, my suspicion was more like wishful thinking and it wasn't the least bit nasty. In fact, it was pretty darn tempting.'

Heat crept along her veins. She bit her bottom lip

in an effort to counter its heavy throbbing. There was nothing she could do about her breasts, though, except to keep her arms tightly folded across them and hope their eager swelling didn't show.

'But I'm severing ties with Bellaroo Creek while you're in the process of establishing them. And while I wouldn't be averse to a purely physical arrangement...'

She shook her head.

'That's what I figured.'

She pulled a breath of fresh country air into her lungs to try to cool her body's unaccountable response to the man opposite; to give herself the space she needed to remember the promises she'd made to herself. 'Romance in any shape or form isn't figuring on my horizon for the next year or two.'

He stared at her, frowned. 'Why not?'

She glanced at Krissie still dozing beneath the lemon tree, and at Ty and Barney wrestling gently in the long grass down by the back fence. 'Because at the moment the children need stability in their lives. Bringing a new man into the mix would freak them out, threaten them.' For the next year or two she meant to focus all her energies on them and what they needed.

For pity's sake! It couldn't be that hard. She'd spent the last twenty-six years focussing on nothing but herself and her music. It wouldn't kill her to put others' needs before her own for a while. In fact, she had a feeling it was mandatory. Anyway, what did she know about romantic relationships? She'd had flirtations, but nothing serious or long-term. She didn't know enough about them to risk Ty's and Krissie's well-being, that was for sure.

'Tess, you're young and beautiful. You're entitled to a life of your own.'

She stared at him. Did he really think she was beautiful?

She started and shook her stupid vanity aside. 'Well, then, hopefully another two years won't make much difference to either of those things.'

'I think you're making a mistake.'

'Ten months,' she shot back. 'I think you're the one making a mistake.'

They glared at each other. 'Speaking of nosy questions…' his glare deepened '…I have one of my own.'

She moistened dry lips. 'Oh?'

He hitched his head in the direction of the children. 'Who hurt them?'

The strength drained from her legs. She reached out but the chicken coop wasn't stable enough to take her weight. She backed up and plonked down on a load of timber Cam had placed to one side, a chasm opening up in her chest. She wanted nothing more than to drop her face to her hands, but if either child glanced her way it would frighten them, worry them, and calming their anxieties was her number-one concern.

Cam swore. She glanced up. With the sun behind her, she could see his face clearly and the range of expressions that filtered across it—concern, protectiveness…anger.

Who hurt them? Her chest cramped. She'd hoped… 'Is it that obvious?' she whispered.

He eased himself down beside her. 'Not at first.'

She had a feeling he was trying to humour her, to offer her some comfort, but there was no comfort to be had. Not for her.

'Tess?'

She chafed her arms as a chill settled over her, although the sun and the air remained warm. 'Their father,' she finally said. 'It was their father.'

From the corner of her eyes she saw one of his hands clench. She sensed that every muscle in his body had tensed. 'He hit them?'

She nodded.

'And he hit their mother?'

She nodded again.

'The bastard!'

She had to swallow a lump at the pointlessness of it all. 'Oh, Cameron, it's so much sadder than that.' Heartbreakingly sad.

'Did he kill their mother and then commit suicide?'

Her head came up at that. 'No!' The police had

been certain. 'It was a car accident.' She swallowed. 'They hit a tree. The police who arrived first on the scene found an injured kangaroo on the road.'

'They swerved to avoid it?'

'I expect so.'

He reached out to clasp one of the hands she had clenched in her lap. 'Tell me the sad story, Tess.'

Why did he want to know? And then she thought about Lorraine, and Lance and Fiona. Maybe something in Sarah and Bruce's story would touch a chord with him. Maybe it would help heal the anger and pain inside him. Maybe it would help him find a way to forgive. Lance might not deserve that forgiveness, but she had a growing certainty that Cam needed to find it inside himself all the same.

His grip tightened and finally she met his gaze. She turned her hand over and without any hesitation at all he entwined his fingers with hers, giving her the silent strength and support she needed.

'As far as I can tell,' she finally started, 'Sarah and Bruce were happy for most of their marriage.' Though God knew she wasn't an expert. 'But two and a half years ago Bruce was involved in an accident at his work where he suffered a brain injury.'

'Where did he work?'

'In an open cut mine in the Upper Hunter Valley. An explosion went off when it shouldn't have. It was all touch and go for a while. He spent four months in hospital and then had months and months of rehabilitation.'

'What happened?' he prompted when she stopped.

She clung to his hand. Unconsciously she leaned one bare arm against his until she remembered that there were still warm good things in the world. 'His personality changed. This previously calm, family-oriented man suddenly had a temper he couldn't control. It would apparently flare up at the smallest provocation.' And then Bruce would lash out with his fists. 'He looked the same, he sounded the same, but he was a totally different man from the one my sister had married.'

'She should've removed the children from that situation immediately.'

Tess stilled. Very gently she removed her hand from his, and went back to chafing her arms. 'We're so quick to judge, aren't we? But how sacred do you hold wedding vows, Cameron? Because my sister took them very seriously. *For better for worse; in sickness and in health.* The accident wasn't Bruce's fault. He didn't go looking for it. He'd simply been in the wrong place at the wrong time. How do you abandon someone who's been through that?' She peered up at him. 'I don't think you'd abandon a woman who'd been through something like that.'

He stared at her and then dragged a hand down his face. 'Did you know about the violence?'

Bitterness filled her mouth and she shook her

head. 'I was hardly ever in the country. I was too busy with my career and gallivanting around Europe and making a name for myself to notice anything.'

She'd been off having the time of her life while her sister had been living a nightmare. Sarah had always been so staunchly independent but that was no excuse. Deep down she'd known something had been troubling her sister, only Sarah would deny it whenever Tess had pressed her. Oh, yes, there had been signs. Signs she hadn't picked up on.

Her vision blurred. Sarah had been so proud of Tess's successes, but they were nothing—surface glitter with no substance. Like Tess herself.

'Tess?'

She shook herself. 'I found out about the violence after the car accident, from Sarah's neighbours and Bruce's doctors. From Ty and Krissie.' And from the letter Sarah had left her, asking her to look after the children if anything should happen to her, and leaving her a ludicrously large life insurance policy, enabling her to do exactly that.

She lifted her chin. 'All that matters now is making sure Ty and Krissie feel safe and building a good life for them here. I'll do whatever that takes.'

'Why?'

The single question chilled her. 'Because I love them.' That was the truth. Cam didn't need to know any more than that. She wasn't sure she could bear the disgust in his eyes if she told him the whole truth.

'Miss Laing, there you are! We've been knocking on the front door, but you obviously didn't hear us.'

Tess and Cam shot to their feet as three women came around the side of the house—Cam's mum, Stacy Bennet and the unknown but well-dressed woman who'd addressed Tess.

Tess urged herself forward and forced what she hoped was a welcoming smile to her lips. 'I'm terribly sorry!'

'It's no matter, dear,' Lorraine said. 'But I want to introduce you to Helen Milton. She's the headmistress of Lachlan Downs Ladies College, which is a boarding school two hours south of here. She's made the trip into Bellaroo Creek especially to meet you.'

Cam rolled his shoulders and remained where he was. Why on earth did Helen want to meet Tess?

'I saw you play when I was in London the year before last. My dear, you have such a rare talent, but it wasn't until I saw you play in Barcelona a few months later that I truly realised it.'

Tess's spine, her shoulders, her whole bearing stiffened. He couldn't see her face, but the fact she made no reply told its own story. He moved to stand beside her.

'Hello, Cameron.'

He glanced down at his mother and his stomach clenched. 'Mum.'

'Oh, no, no, no,' Helen continued, 'you won't be hiding your light under a bushel out here, Tess!'

Tess gripped her hands together, her knuckles turning white. 'Oh, but—'

'You don't mind me calling you Tess, do you?'

'Of course not. I—'

'It'd be a crime for you to bury your talent and I won't allow it.'

Lorraine smiled at him and behind the lines of strain that fanned out from her eyes he recognised genuine delight. 'Tess is apparently not just a world-class pianist, but a classical guitarist of some note too.'

He stared at her. Not a dancer but a musician? It made perfect sense. It explained her innate grace and balance, and the way her whole being came alive when she sang.

She shrugged, colour flooding her cheeks as he continued to stare at her. He nudged her arm. 'Tess, that's really something.'

But she stared back at him with doe-in-the-head-light eyes and he didn't understand, only knew something was terribly wrong. He straightened. 'How about we go inside and I'll put the kettle on?' Tess needed something warm and sweet inside her.

'I can't, I'm sorry—this is just a flying visit. I need to be back at the college by three—I've chartered a plane—but I wanted to introduce myself to Tess while I had a brief window of opportunity.' Helen turned back to Tess. 'Because I have plans for you, my dear.'

'Oh?' Tess's voice was nothing but a whisper.

'Every year we hold a two-week summer camp at the college, and we want you to give music tuition. Heavens, talk about a coup!'

'But…but I couldn't possibly leave Ty and Krissie for two whole weeks.'

'My dear, they can come too. There'll be all sorts of activities to keep them occupied.'

'But—'

Helen's eyes narrowed and hardened. Cam shifted his feet. The headmistress hadn't got where she was today by taking no for an answer.

'Miss Laing, you can't possibly have a problem with wanting to assist the community that has taken you under its wing. Surely?'

'Well, no, of course not.'

His lips twisted. The rotten woman should've gone into politics.

'Excellent!' She took Tess's arm and led her back the way she'd come. 'I'll email you with all the details. And don't worry, you'll be handsomely reimbursed.'

'How are you, Cameron?' his mother asked, her question stopping him from following.

He rolled his shoulders. 'Fine, and you?'

Her hand fluttered to her throat. 'Fine.'

He shifted from one leg to the other. 'Would you like to come around for dinner one day this week?' The words burst from him. They burned and needled but he didn't retract them.

'Oh!' She swallowed. 'I...I'm afraid this week isn't good.'

'Right.' Exactly the same response as the last time he'd asked her. 'Let me know when your diary clears.'

She opened her mouth, but closed it again without saying anything more. 'I'd better go,' she finally said. 'Goodbye, Cameron.'

'Mum.'

He stared after her and then started in surprise when Ty slipped his small hand inside Cam's. He glanced down. 'You okay, buddy?'

'What did that lady want?'

'I think she wants your auntie Tess to do some work for her.'

'Auntie Tess didn't look very happy.'

No, she hadn't. Why not? If she had a passion for music... Cam cut the thought off and focused on allaying Ty's concern instead. 'I think your auntie Tess is going to be just fine, Ty. She doesn't have to do anything she doesn't want to.'

Ty thought about that for a moment and then nodded. 'Would you like to play fetch with Barney?'

CHAPTER FIVE

Cam strode through the back door of the school-house. If Stacy really wanted to turn that lower field into a play area for the children, they were going to need to talk about drainage, fund-raising and working bees.

He turned the corner and then pulled up short as Tess bolted through the school's front door.

He swallowed. He'd spent two afternoons last week finishing off the chicken coop. Both times she'd invited him to stay for dinner. Both times he'd declined. Since he'd revealed he was leaving Bellaroo Creek, they'd maintained a polite but slightly formal distance.

Which was fine by him. As far as he was concerned the less time he spent thinking about her, the better.

He watched her halt now, press her hands to her waist and drag in a breath. Something was up. Before he could kick himself forward and ask what, she'd set her spine and moved straight for Stacy Bennet's office. 'Hey, chickadee, what's up?'

Before she could enter the office, however, Krissie had hurtled out of it to fling herself at Tess, her face crumpled and her shoulders shaking with sobs. Tess held her against her with one hand while the other caressed the hair back off her face. His gut tightened as he watched her. Her love was evident in every touch and gesture. The set of her shoulders and her bent head told him that Krissie's pain was her own. He had to swallow. He rolled his shoulders, but he couldn't look away.

Krissie's storm was brief. When she finally relaxed her grip, Tess led her back into the office. Had someone frightened Krissie again? Almost without thinking he moved towards the office, halting in its doorway. Tess, Krissie and Stacy all sat on Stacy's sofa, and Tess wiped Krissie's face with a handful of tissues. They didn't see him.

'You want to tell me what happened, chickadee?'

He marvelled at the calm strength in her voice, at her distinct I-can-fix-anything attitude. He shoved his hands in his pockets. Tess Laing was a hell of a woman. He took a step back. She obviously had everything under control. He should leave and give them some privacy. He turned away.

'Do we have money troubles?' Krissie hiccupped.

He stiffened and swung back.

'Heavens, no,' Tess pooh-poohed. 'What's brought this on?'

'Mikey said we must be poor if we're renting a house for a dollar a week. And I know that when you're poor bad things can happen.'

Cam stiffened. A five-year-old should be happy and carefree, not constantly glancing over her shoulder waiting for bad things to happen. A five-year-old shouldn't have so little faith in all that was bright and good.

Neither should a twenty-nine-year-old.

He shook that thought off.

For the first time he truly appreciated the task Tess had set herself.

Tess tucked the child under her arm and pulled her in close. 'When you're a bit older I'll explain life insurance policies to you, chickadee. You'll probably learn all about them at school when you're fourteen or fifteen. But I can promise—cross my heart—that your mum and dad made sure that you, Ty and me would have enough money so we wouldn't want for anything.'

She'd taken the perfect tone, and she had perfect—

He averted his gaze and wished he'd thought to do that before she'd crossed her heart.

He glanced back to see Krissie turn up a hopeful face. 'Really?'

'Really, truly.'

'Daddy too?'

'Daddy too.'

Tess might've taken the perfect tone, but some sixth sense warned him that she was horribly close to tears. Stacy jumped to the rescue. 'You want to know why your aunt Tess wanted to come to Bellaroo Creek, Krissie?'

She stared up at the teacher with solemn eyes and nodded.

'It's because she knew we wanted you all to come and live out here and be a part of our town. Your aunt Tess knows how nice it is to be wanted.'

The child swung to Tess and Tess smiled at her. 'It's true. Don't you think it's lovely to come to a place where everyone wants to be friends with us? And weren't we talking just last night about all the things we like about living in Bellaroo Creek?'

'You like the fresh air.'

'I sure do.' She nudged Krissie's shoulder with a grin. 'And I'm finding I have a big soft spot for sultana cake.'

Krissie giggled. 'And I love Fluffy and Ty loves Barney. And Louisa and Suzie are really nice, and so is Mrs Bennet,' she added with a shy glance at her teacher.

'So you don't need to get upset about anything anyone says, all right?' Tess said.

Krissie pursed her lips and finally nodded, obviously deciding to trust her aunt. 'Okay.'

'How about you run back to class now, Krissie?' her teacher said. 'Mrs Leigh is teaching everyone a new song and you wouldn't want to miss out on that, would you?'

With a hug for Tess, Krissie started for the door. Cam suddenly realised he still stood there staring. He tried to duck out of the way, but he wasn't quick enough. 'Cam!' Krissie hugged him, grinning up at him with those big brown eyes of hers before disappearing down the corridor to her classroom.

He gulped and turned back to Tess and Stacy. 'Sorry, I was coming in to talk to you about that lower field. I didn't mean…'

'Well, as you're here now you may as well come in.' Stacy waved him in as she walked back behind her desk. 'You've obviously become good friends with your new neighbours if Krissie's reaction is anything to go by.'

The collar of his shirt tightened. He didn't know what to say, so he entered the room and sat on the sofa beside Tess, careful to keep a safe distance between them. 'You okay?' he murmured.

'Sure.' Tess sent him a wan smile before turning back to Stacy. 'Mrs Bennet, I'm so sorry. I—'

'Stacy, dear, please…at least when the children aren't present. And let me assure you there's no need to apologise. There were always going to be a few teething problems. I knew that the moment I read your application and discovered Ty and Krissie had recently lost their parents.'

Tess's breath whooshed out of her. 'That didn't put you off accepting us into town?'

'Absolutely not! We think you're perfect for Bella-roo Creek. And we think our town has a lot to offer all of you too. What are a few teething problems in the grand scheme, anyway? So don't you go making this bigger in your mind than it ought to be. The children will settle in just fine, you'll see. What we need to do now is sort you out.'

'Me?' she squeaked.

'But before we move on to that, I just want to let you know that if Krissie has another little outburst like that, then we'll deal with it in-house rather than calling you in.'

'Oh, but—'

'Believe me, Tess, it'll be for the best. I thought it important you came today, just so Krissie knows she can rely on you, but from hereon we'll deal with it.'

'But what if—?'

Stacy held up a hand and Cam heard Tess literally swallow. 'Oh, I'm making a hash of it, aren't I?'

His jaw dropped. He turned to her. 'What are you talking about? You've been brilliant!'

'Cam is right, Tess. You're doing a remarkable job in difficult circumstances. I sincerely applaud all you've achieved.'

Tess shot him a glance before turning back to Stacy. Her spine straightened. 'Thank you.'

'Believe me, you can be the natural mother of twelve children and still feel utterly clueless some days.'

Tess stared, and then she started to laugh. 'I'm not sure that's particularly comforting, but it makes me feel better all the same.' She leant forward, her hands clasped on her knees. 'Okay, so what did you mean when you said you needed to sort me out?'

'Do you really think you'll find it satisfying enough just keeping house and looking after the children?'

'Well, I—'

'My dear, I think you'll go mad. So what I want to propose is for you to run a class or two for our OOSH programme.'

'OOSH?'

'Out of school hours,' Stacy clarified. 'The classes would only run for forty minutes or so. The school has a budget for it, so you would be paid.'

Tess opened her mouth, but no sound came out.

'It'll be a great benefit to the community during term time and great for the kids. More important, however, I expect it will help keep you fresh and stop you from going stir crazy.'

Tess stiffened when she realised exactly what kind of classes Stacy was going to ask her to teach—music classes. Cam stared at her and recalled the way she'd tensed up when Helen had co-opted her for the summer school. He frowned. Surely with her experience and expertise teaching music classes would be a cinch. If she had a passion for music, wouldn't she be eager to share it?

He didn't want to ask any awkward questions. At least, not in front of Stacy, but...

Silence stretched throughout the office. Finally Tess smoothed back her hair. 'I know you're thinking of my piano and guitar training,' she said quietly. Too quietly. 'But piano isn't really appropriate to teach to a large group. As for guitar, that will only work if everyone has their own instrument.'

Stacy grimaced and shook her head.

Tess's hands relaxed their ferocious grip on each other. He stared at them, and then opened his mouth. He could donate the funds needed to buy the school guitars.

'I figured that might be the case,' Tess said.

He closed his mouth again, curious to see what she meant to propose.

She pursed her lips and pretended to consider the problem. He stared, trying to work out how he knew it was a pretence, but he couldn't put a finger on it. He kept getting sidetracked by the perfect colour of her skin and the plump promise of her lips.

'I could do percussion classes,' she said. 'It teaches timing and rhythm and the kids would love it.'

'Sounds...noisy,' he said.

'Which no doubt is part of the fun,' said Stacy. 'What equipment would you need?'

'Any kind of percussion instrument the school or the children have lying around—drums, cymbals, triangles, maracas, clappers. Even two bits of wood would work, or rice in a plastic milk container.'

'We can make some of those in class.'

'Do you have recorders?' Both he and Stacy groaned. Tess grinned. 'I'll take that as a yes. In my opinion recorders get a bad rap. They're a wonderful tool for teaching children how to read music.'

'Oh, Tess, that sounds perfect!' Stacy clasped her hands on her desk and beamed at them. 'Can you start next week? We hold the classes at the community hall and there'll always be a parent or four to help out. Would Tuesdays and Thursdays suit you?'

'I'd love to be involved, and any day of the week is fine with me.'

Cam couldn't tell if she truly meant it or not, but he sensed her sincere desire to fit in, to become fully involved in life at Bellaroo Creek. To give back. His stomach rolled. While he was intent on leaving.

'I know you're busy on Kurrajong, Cam, but I don't suppose you'd take a class?'

He went to say, You can take that right, when Krissie's crumpled face rose in his mind…along with the way Ty flinched whenever he was startled as if waiting for a blow to fall. 'I'll teach judo classes on a Wednesday if you think there'll be any takers.'

Tess spun to him. He refused to look at her. He refused to consider too deeply what that meant for his plans. It'd only be a minor delay. It'd only mean hanging around in Bellaroo Creek for an extra month to six weeks. He did what he could to stop his lip from curling.

'I forgot you had judo training. You received your training certificate before you went off to university, didn't you?'

He nodded. Teaching judo had helped pay his way through university.

'Excellent! That'll be another winner. I can't tell you both how much I appreciate it. I'll be in touch to fine-tune the details,' Stacy said. 'Now, Cam, my lower field.'

'We need to talk drainage and fund-raising.'

She sighed. 'Just as I feared. We might have to leave that all for another day,' she said, leading them to the door. 'But many thanks for coming out here and taking a look. Take care, the both of you.'

Cam glanced at Tess as they set off for the front gate. Was she all right? Dealing with Krissie's and Ty's fears and insecurities had to be taking its toll. He didn't doubt for a moment that she loved them, but... She'd essentially gone from fêted musician to a single mother of two needy children in the blink of an eye. It couldn't be easy. Some days it must be bloody heartbreaking and exhausting. 'Are you okay?'

One shoulder lifted, but lines of fatigue fanned out from her eyes. 'Sure.' When he didn't say anything she glanced up, grimaced and shrugged again. 'Some days it feels as if we take one step forward and three steps back.'

He couldn't think of anything to say that didn't sound like a platitude or the accepted wisdom she already knew.

'I know it'll get better with time.'

But how much time? And how ragged would she run herself in the meantime? He glanced at her again and bit back a curse.

'You did that for Ty's and Krissie's sakes, didn't you?' she said, when they reached their cars. She blinked in the sunlight. 'Offering to teach judo.'

He chose his words carefully. 'I think if they feel they can defend themselves, they'll become a little more…relaxed.'

'I don't doubt that for a single moment, but…'

But? He shifted. 'I don't teach fighting as a good or positive thing to do, Tess. Judo is about self-discipline and learning how to defend yourself.'

'Oh, it's not that!' She actually looked shocked by the idea. 'But…' she glanced around as if afraid of being overheard '…I thought you were leaving town?'

He rolled his shoulders. 'I am. That hasn't changed.' He wanted them very clear on that. 'But there's still a lot of work to sort out on Kurrajong. Hanging around until the end of the school term means I won't be leaving it all for my station manager to sort out.' He gritted his teeth. What was a month?

Besides, it had struck him afresh in Stacy's office that while he was fighting not to turn into his father, that was exactly what he was in danger of becoming. Just like his father, he'd withdrawn from the community and thrown himself into work on the station. Leaving Bellaroo Creek and involving himself in a cause he was passionate about would ensure that history didn't repeat, but in the meantime he had to fight that inward impulse as much as he could. Even if it meant coming face-to-face with Lance and Fiona some time in the near future.

What would that matter? In three months he'd be in Africa.

In the meantime, he would not bury himself on Kurrajong Station with all of his bitterness and shattered dreams. He thrust his shoulders back. He'd get the chance to explore new horizons, stretch his wings, and shake the dust of this godforsaken place from his boots soon enough.

'You know, I'd kill for a piece of butter cake with orange icing right about now.'

He blinked himself back into the present. 'Sorry, Tess, I'm afraid the town doesn't stretch to a bakery.' Though rumour had it that might change in the not too distant future with Milla Brady coming home. One could only hope.

'It doesn't mean I can't make a cake of my own, though.'

True enough. He opened her car door for her. 'You think it'll cheer Krissie up?'

'It may well do,' she said with a shrug, but a cheeky grin peeped through. 'Mostly I just want one because I'm famished!'

He laughed, noting the way her shoulders had started to loosen.

'I don't know what it is about the air out here, but my appetite suddenly seems to know no bounds.'

'Will you have time for a lesson on the lawn-mower this afternoon? It's in perfect working order again and I thought I might bring it over.' It occurred to him that it might be a good idea for Tess to have company this afternoon.

'Oh, that'll be perfect! I'll feed you cake, and you can teach me the fine art of lawnmower riding.'

'Deal.'

He tried to ignore the excitement that curled in his stomach as she drove away. He was teaching her how to use the ride-on, that was all. If he was lucky it might stop her from brooding. End of story.

Cam drove the mower into the backyard. From her position at the kitchen window Tess's gaze zeroed in on those impressive shoulders and the strongly defined muscles of his upper arms, and her breath hitched.

She leaned closer to get a better look. She fanned her face. She jumped when the oven timer dinged.

She wrenched her gaze away. It had been an emotional morning. This was a carry-over reaction from that. She shied away from the 'emotional' part of that thought too. It made her insides start to wobble again, and she was getting tired of wobbling, of feeling the ground constantly shifting beneath her feet.

'Come on through,' she hollered before he could knock on the back door.

She pulled the cake from the oven and, although she sensed him standing behind her, she set the cake on the bench and just stared at it, her mouth watering. She needed to let it cool for at least ten minutes before cutting into it.

Longer if she intended to ice it.

When she finally turned to Cam, his lips twitched as if he could read her hunger, her greed. He nodded towards it, his eyes dancing. 'I'm impressed.'

Something in his voice… Didn't he think that she could bake? She stuck her nose in the air. 'So you should be.'

Then she grinned. 'I've been practising becoming model-mother material since before we left Sydney.' She tapped an old exercise book—Sarah's recipe book—her sister's handwriting as familiar as her own. 'There's a wealth of hints and tips in this baby.'

'What is it?'

She handed it to him, and then hitched her head in

the direction of the yard, grabbing her sunhat as they went. 'C'mon, I'm dying to eat cake so the sooner I learn all I need to about your ride-on mower, the better.'

Barney greeted them with excited barks, leaping up on Tess and practically exploding with delight when she petted him. Fluffy followed behind at a far more dignified pace.

'C'mon, you two.' She scooped the puppy up in one hand and the chicken in her other and popped them both in the chicken mansion out of harm's way. They proceeded to romp down the length of the run together.

Cam stared. 'Who'd have believed it? They've become playmates.'

'I'm convinced Fluffy thinks she's a dog. I'm not sure what she's going to do when we get more chickens.'

'When are you planning on that?'

'Just as soon as I do my research and know what I'm doing.' The last thing she needed was a dead chicken or three. There'd been enough death in the children's lives—and hers—to last them for a lifetime.

'I've some books you can borrow.'

'Thanks, but I have a couple on order at the library.'

Bellaroo Creek had the tiniest library on the planet—full of fat romance novels of which she'd fully availed herself. As part of the Greater Parkes Shire, though, the library had a huge range of books available through the inter-library loan scheme. Her books should arrive within the week.

Cam surveyed her. 'You don't want to accept my help?'

She recalled the heat that had hit her at the kitchen window, the silly flutter in her chest. 'It's not that. It's just the library already has them on order for me.' And she was *not* going to get into the habit of counting on Cam too much. Not when he was leaving Bellaroo Creek. Not when he heated her blood so quickly and assailed her senses so fully she found it impossible to keep her balance around him.

She dragged her gaze from the green promise of his eyes and gestured to the mower. 'What do I need to know?'

He placed Sarah's book on the garden bench Tess and the children had hauled around from the front yard last weekend, and gestured to the mower. 'C'mon, then, up you get.'

He helped her climb on and his hand on her arm was warm and strong. Absurdly, it made her feel strong too.

'Okay, quick overview—handbrake, foot brake and accelerator—' he pointed to each of them '—and this lever here—' he tapped it '—lifts and lowers the cutting blades.'

'Right.' She nodded. It was an auto transmission—easy-peasy.

'People generally run into two problems with ride-ons. The first is stalling the mower because they're trying to set off too fast. The second is setting the cutter blades too low and hitting dirt. So let's work on starting it up and moving forwards first. Ignition is right there.' He handed her a key.

She fitted it to the ignition and it started up first go. She put her foot on the brake, let out the handbrake and then pressed down on the accelerator.

And stalled.

Cam didn't laugh. He just reached over and pulled the handbrake on, hitting her with his heat and the scent of cut grass. 'Okay, let's try that again.'

Even though her heart beat faster, his calm confidence filtered into her.

'Ease your foot gently onto the accelerator.'

She did as he instructed and this time the mower edged forward. She drove to the lemon tree before pulling to a halt again, a ludicrous flush of accomplishment surging through her. She grinned as he strode up to her and he grinned back. It suddenly struck her how sunny it was out here, how clear the sky and how good everything smelled.

He taught her how to reverse. He showed her how to adjust the blade level. 'Okay, show me what you're made of, Tess Laing. Off you go. I want to see you do a lap around the chicken coop.'

She took a deep breath and headed for the chicken coop. She finished the lap, headed for the back fence and then did it all over again.

'Yee ha!' Holding her hat to her head, she lifted her face to the sun and laughed for the sheer joy of it. Who knew a ride-on lawnmower could be so much fun? 'Oh, man, I have to get me one of these!'

She clamped both hands back to the steering wheel as she whizzed around the chicken coop a third time. Barney raced the length of the chicken run beside her, barking madly and wagging his tail. Cam laughed at her, but she didn't mind in the least. This—this mad, fun dash on the mower—felt like freedom.

With the kids having started school this week, she'd started to feel less tense, less…shackled. Until this morning, that was. But…to not have to be on her guard all the time, aware that her every move and word could impact on Ty and Krissie in some unforseen way. That…well, it was heaven.

Not that she didn't miss the children being at home with her, but she relished the downtime from them too. Nobody had told her how much mess they could make, or how noisy they could be, or how grumpy they could get when they were tired or… or just how relentless parenthood was.

And nobody had warned her how much that could take out of a person.

Which went to show what a poor substitute she was for Sarah.

She promptly stalled the mower.

Cam came up, a frown in his eyes. 'What happened?'

She swallowed. 'I, uh, lost my concentration for a moment.' She tried to find that elusive sense of freedom again, but it slipped out of reach. 'Thank you for the lesson, Cameron. I think I have the hang of it now.' She started the mower up again. Something in his eyes made the ache inside her threaten to explode, and she wasn't sure if tears or heat would be the outcome—and she had no intention of finding out. 'I'll just park it up near the house.' She didn't wait for him to say anything, but took off.

She climbed off the mower and checked her watch.

'Somewhere you need to be?'

She suddenly laughed. 'I'm just waiting for that darn cake to cool. I'd planned on icing it, but I'm not sure I can wait that long. I'll put the kettle on in a moment and cut us both a slice. I just want to check the animals' water first.'

Cam settled on the garden bench and picked up Sarah's book. Tess checked the water bowl by the back door and then the one in the chicken coop, letting Barney and Fluffy out to play in the yard.

Cam gave a sudden snort. 'You have got to be joking! Listen to this. "Carrot spaghetti: using a vegetable peeler, create long lengths of carrot to look like spaghetti. Submerge in boiling water for a few seconds and then top with pasta sauce. Children will love it and it's a tasty way to ensure they eat their vegetables.'"

She nodded. 'I know. Who has the time for that, huh? Do you know how long it takes to peel a whole carrot with a vegetable peeler?'

He stared at her. The book dropped to his lap. 'You've tried this?'

'Well…' She heaved back a sigh. 'I just never knew it could be so hard to get kids to eat their veggies. There's loads more tips in there about grating carrot and zucchini and adding it to mince when making rissoles or meatloaf…and grating cauliflower and zucchini into hash-brown mixture and…'

She plonked down beside him. 'Long gone are the days of pulling a frozen dinner out of the freezer and nuking it in the microwave.' And God help her, but she missed those days. A sigh overtook her. 'Do you know how long it takes to grate anything?'

'Hell, Tess.'

She straightened. 'I mean, that's one of the reasons we came out here—so I'd have plenty of time to do exactly that.' Looking after Ty and Krissie was the most important job in the world to her, so what were a few grated carrots between family, huh?

'You're going to send yourself around the twist grating vegetables as if there's no tomorrow.'

It was starting to feel that way, but...

'You know what, Tess?'

She glanced at him and the sympathy and compassion in his eyes made her sinuses burn and her throat ache. 'What?' she whispered.

'I think you need to stop trying to be Sarah and focus on being yourself.'

Her head rocked back.

'And another thing... Why are you so reluctant to continue with your music?'

She froze.

'Why aren't you eager to dive back into your piano and guitar?'

An invisible hand reached inside her chest to squeeze her heart.

'Hasn't it occurred to you that playing again might actually help you manage all your stress and worry?'

'No!' She leapt up. 'You're wrong. So wrong!'

She stood there, hands clenched, shaking, and realised too late how utterly revealing her reaction had been. She forced herself to sit again, doing what she could to hide her panic. 'No.' She moderated her tone. 'You don't understand.'

'Then explain it to me.'

Explain? Oh, that was impossible, but... 'Music consumes me. I... When I play, nothing else matters. For the time being, it needs to go on the backburner until I get a decent handle on my new life.'

All true, but she couldn't look at him as she said it.

He surveyed her for a long moment. It took a superhuman effort not to fidget. 'So you haven't played since you heard about Sarah's accident?'

The yearning rose within her but she ruthlessly smothered it. 'There hasn't been time.' There would never be time. She'd make sure of it. She'd turned her back on that life of selfishness.

His eyes suddenly narrowed. 'Why do I get the feeling you're punishing yourself?'

'Low blood sugar,' she prescribed, jumping up. 'It's beyond time I serve up that promised cake.'

'Tess.'

She halted halfway to the back door and then turned. 'Cam, can we leave this for now? I…I just need to get my priorities straight and my music messes with that too much. I'll sort it out eventually, but in the meantime talking about it doesn't help.'

She hated lying to him. But he was leaving Bellaroo Creek soon and… And it was just too hard.

With a nod, he let it be and she could've hugged him. To stop from doing anything so stupid, she set up the card table and served tea and cake. Cam ate it with the same relish as she did, and it lifted something inside her.

Eventually they both sat back, sated.

'Tess, about grating all those vegetables.'

His tone made her laugh. 'Yes?'

'I don't think it's necessary.'

'No? Well, c'mon, convince me, because, believe me, if I never see another grated carrot for as long as I live it'll be too soon.'

He sobered, that compassion alive in his eyes again. 'Tess, no matter what you do you'll never be able to make up to Krissie and Ty that they've lost their parents. You can grate from now till kingdom come, but it won't make a scrap of difference.'

Her throat closed over.

'And spoiling them in the attempt will be doing them a grave disservice.'

With a superhuman effort, she swallowed. Had she been spoiling them? 'You think I fuss over them too much, don't you?'

His face softened. 'I think when you're feeling more confident, you'll relax a bit more.'

'So…that's a yes, then?'

He remained silent.

She pondered what he'd said. It should break her heart that she couldn't make up to Ty and Krissie that they'd lost their parents. And it did, but it was strangely freeing too. It gave her permission to focus on the things she could change.

She glanced at Cam. He'd put his exciting plans for Africa on hold for a whole additional month for Krissie and Ty…and for her. She started to smile. 'You're saying I'll never have to grate another carrot in my life?'

'That's exactly what I'm saying.'

He grinned back at her and she couldn't help it. She leaned across and pressed her lips to his.

CHAPTER SIX

CAM DIDN'T PULL away. He didn't even hesitate. He greeted Tess's kiss with wholehearted pleasure. One of his hands cupped her face, engulfing her in his warmth. Tendrils of sensation unfurled in her stomach and drifted out to every corner of her body in slow adagios of delight. Waltzing delight.

And then the tendrils became licks of fire. Cam's free hand curved around the back of her neck and he pulled her in closer, his lips moving over hers more fully, more thoroughly, offering her even more delight, making her even hungrier for him.

Greedy to taste, greedy to touch, she slid her hands to either side of his face and she explored the texture of his jaw and the strong column of his neck until her hands and fingers were as alive as her lips. When he licked the corner of her mouth, traced the fullness of her bottom lip, she opened up to him and he dragged her right into his lap as their tongues danced. She wound her arms about his neck as if she never meant to let him go.

She gave herself up to the thrill of being alive and in his arms. Kissing Cameron was like listening to vibrant, wonderful music. Better yet, it was like *making* vibrant, wonderful music. Music that could fill the soul and send it soaring free, and Tess wanted to soar and fly and swoop and twirl with Cameron and never stop.

She slipped her hand between the buttons of his shirt, needing to touch firm bare skin. His hand slid beneath her shirt, his caress an omen of bliss. And then they both stilled, so unaccountably in tune with each other that they knew.

They knew this had become more than a kiss. It was about to become something a whole lot more interesting…if that was what they chose.

If.

Tess stared up into eyes so vivid with promise that all she had to do was reach out. She sucked her bottom lip into her mouth and tasted him there. Her body clamoured for more, but…

She shivered. Ty and Krissie.

She gave a tiny shake of her head.

She felt the sigh he heaved back, but he nodded his acknowledgement. He went to lift her off his lap, but she held up a hand to forestall him. She dragged in a breath, counted to three…four, and then removed herself under her own steam until she was sitting beside him again.

'I really shouldn't have done that,' she murmured.

He surveyed her with watchful eyes, but didn't say anything. She bit her lip and then shrugged. 'But while I shouldn't have kissed you, I can't find it in myself to be sorry for it.' She frowned, suddenly realising how selfish that sounded. 'I mean, I'm sorry if I made you—'

'Me neither, Tess,' he cut in.

He leaned back, a grin lighting those ecstasy-inducing lips of his and hunger raged through her.

'I don't see why you shouldn't have done it. I don't have a problem if you want to do it again.' He raised his hands. 'Just saying.'

She laughed and shook her head. 'I shouldn't have done it because I liked it too much.'

'And there's a problem with that?'

It was the same as when she played the piano or the guitar—the world receded and the music took over. And until three months ago, she'd let it. Willingly. Gladly. She'd welcomed it. Only now, she knew how selfish that had been. How unfair it had been to those around her.

No more.

She'd let her selfish obsession keep her from Sarah, when her sister had needed her. She couldn't afford to let Ty and Krissie down in the same way.

'There are just too many strikes against us, Cameron.'

'Like?'

'Like the fact I truly believe Ty and Krissie need

stability for a while. I don't think it's fair to ask them to adjust to a new man in their lives just yet. Not after everything they've been through. I don't think that's unreasonable, even if you do. We're just searching for…'

'An even keel.'

She nodded. 'I really don't want to mess this up.'

'Strike One,' he murmured.

She glanced down at her hands and then back at him. 'There are other issues too. You have a grudge in your heart that's bigger than forty hectares of golden canola. Until you come to terms with that, there'll never be room in your heart for another woman.'

He drew back. 'I have good reason for that grudge.'

'Yes, you do.'

'But?'

Couldn't he see how much his bitterness, how much holding on to his grudge was hurting him? 'It's just from where I'm standing—sitting—that's Strike Two.'

He didn't say anything.

She couldn't let it go. 'What Lance and Fiona did to you, Cameron, sucks. But…' She gripped her hands together. 'But has it never occurred to you that maybe they never meant for it to happen, that they never meant to hurt you? That maybe they just fell in love with each other? Maybe he's just as appalled by what's happened as you are.'

Cam dragged a hand back through his hair, making it stand on end. She ached to reach out and smooth it back down.

'Look, Tess, all his life Lance has been jealous of me. Jealous that I had a father with a bigger station than his father's. Jealous that I had two homes I divided my time between. Jealous that I did well at sport and at school. You name it—if it was mine, he wanted it.'

He scowled out at the yard. 'If he spent half as much time working towards whatever it was he wanted instead of resenting me for having it, or stealing it from me, then he might have achieved something worthwhile. I thought he'd grow out of it. Hoped he would. For heaven's sake, he's twenty-six years old! I never thought he would go to such lengths, but...'

His hands clenched. 'But it appears he still wants what I have, so, no, I haven't considered the fact that he never meant to hurt me. I know that's precisely what he was hoping to achieve.'

Bile burned the back of Tess's throat at the expression in his eyes.

'He stole all that I most cherished in this world, and he laughed while he did it. Forgiveness, even if he asked for it...'

He broke off, his face growing grimmer. 'This time he went too far. He involved an innocent third party in his nasty little games.'

All that I most cherished. She swallowed, suddenly nauseous. 'Fiona?' The name croaked out of her.

He gave one hard nod.

She swallowed again. 'Forgive me for saying this, but the fact she, um…canoodled with your brother while engaged to you doesn't exactly cast her in the role of an innocent.'

Did he still love that tall, slim woman with the golden ponytail? The thought left a bad taste in her mouth. If her stomach hadn't been churning so badly she'd have grabbed another piece of cake to override it.

'Lance has always had more charm than was good for him. He knows how to woo a woman and make her believe he's in love with her.'

She leant towards him, though she was careful not to touch him. 'But maybe he really loves Fiona.'

He turned to her then and raised a dark eyebrow. 'When he's finished with her, he'll dump her.' His lips compressed into a hard, grim line. 'He'll break her heart. All just to get back at me.'

That didn't ring true. Oh, she didn't doubt for a moment that Cam believed it, but… 'They looked very together at the luncheon…as in a definite couple. Cameron, it's been ten months. Your mother obviously thinks they mean to marry.'

He didn't say anything for a long moment. 'Even

if what you say is true, does that excuse the fact that they betrayed me?'

'Of course it doesn't! But maybe it'd prove that they never meant to hurt you, and that has to count for something.'

'If it were true, perhaps it would.'

She ached for him then, for the pain she sensed bubbling beneath the surface, his utter sense of betrayal. Forgiveness would bring him peace, if only he would consider it. Ten months. Surely that was long enough. But some wounds, she knew, never healed.

She smoothed her hair back, longing to make him smile. 'Do you know you kiss like an angel, Cameron? And that by holding onto your grudge you're depriving some woman out there of the most divine kisses, all because you won't forgive Lance?'

He stared and then a laugh shot out of him. 'I didn't realise you could be quite so persistent.'

'Dog with a bone,' she agreed. Speaking of dogs... She glanced around and then blew out a breath when she found Barney and Fluffy sunning themselves only a few feet away. 'My parents found it one of my less endearing traits.' But it was the reason she'd become such a fine musician.

He leaned towards her, swamping her with his green-grass freshness and all that false promise. She gulped. He didn't mean to kiss her again, did he?

He reached out and traced a finger down her

cheek. Her pulse leapt to life beneath it. 'Tess, regardless of what anyone says, you are divine.'

What if she channelled all the energy she'd put into her music into healing this man, into loving him and showing him there was a better way? Would she succeed? Would she—?

She drew back. She didn't have the time or the luxury for those kinds of games. If she only had herself to consider…

But she didn't.

Her skin pimpled with gooseflesh when she recalled the kind of family Sarah had dreamed of having—a wonderful, close-knit family who loved each other, supported each other and did things together. That had all been taken away from her. It had all gone so terribly wrong for her, and for Ty and Krissie too. Tess couldn't let it go bad for them again. Her fingers shook and her throat tightened. She'd failed Sarah once, but she wouldn't fail her again.

Ty and Krissie were the ones who deserved—who needed—all her energy. And she couldn't risk their hearts to such an endeavour. She couldn't let them become so dependent on Cam that they'd be crushed when he left.

When he left…

'And Strike Three,' she said, 'you're planning on leaving town. Unless you've changed your mind on that head.' Her heart gave a traitorous jump.

'I haven't changed my mind.' He stared down at his hands. 'Strike Three,' he agreed.

They sat in silence for a moment. 'So lots of reasons not to kiss,' he said, as if double-checking her resolve.

'Yep.' She couldn't keep the glumness from her voice.

Cam rose. 'I think it's beyond time that I made tracks.'

A protest clamoured through her but she bit it back. He was right.

He set his dusty Akubra on top of his head and touched its brim in a kind of salute. 'I'll be seeing you, Tess.'

It had all the finality of an irrevocable goodbye.

'Let's go down this road,' Ty said, pointing to the right.

Krissie nodded her agreement.

Ty held Barney on his lap, Krissie held Fluffy on her lap, and Tess had a picnic hamper on the passenger seat beside her. It was Saturday. The children had completed their first full week of school, and they'd agreed to spend the day exploring the surrounds of their new home.

Tess turned the car obediently in the direction Ty had indicated. All the roads around here seemed to be unsealed, and some of them weren't in the best of repair. This one was no exception, but she didn't mind driving slowly to avoid the worst of the potholes and corrugations. It gave her a chance to enjoy the scenery.

And the scenery was stunning—long stretches of low hills green with wheat and lucerne. Here and there a river or stream gleamed silver-blue amid the landscape. There were ridges of land dotted with scribbly gums and sheep, and brown fields enclosing brown cattle, muddy dams and dandelions. It was warm enough still to leave the window down and the air was fresh and green, if occasionally dusty.

'Fluffy thinks that'd be the best spot for our picnic,' Krissie announced, pointing to a stand of Kurrajong trees up ahead.

The trees formed a natural glade that sloped down to a river. Tess glanced at her watch. They'd been driving for just over an hour, and, if her sense of direction was anything to go by, they should've nearly completed the loop that would take them back into Bellaroo Creek.

They'd taken the road west out of town and the plan had been to circle around and come back in on the town's northern side. According to her calculations, they couldn't be more than a couple of kilometres from the township.

And it was nearly lunchtime.

And she was starving!

She pulled the car to the side of the road. 'Well spotted, Fluffy. This looks like a fabulous picnic spot.' She hoped whoever owned the land wouldn't mind them trespassing. 'Watch out for cows,' she hollered as the children and animals spilled from the car and raced towards the river. 'And don't get too close to the water!'

She was out of breath when she reached them. And, truly, it was the prettiest spot. They all gazed at it in silence for a moment as if to just drink it in. 'Beautiful,' Tess breathed.

Krissie slipped her hand inside Tess's. 'Do you think Cam has a river on his station?'

'I haven't the foggiest, chickadee, but I expect so. You can ask him next time you see him.'

'At judo class!'

Both children were excited by the after-school activities on offer, but especially Cam's judo class.

'Ninja!' Ty executed a high, flying kick that made Fluffy flap her wings.

'Food,' Tess countered.

They spread out a blanket and devoured their picnic—sandwiches, fruit, date scones and bottles of water—sharing it all with Barney and Fluffy. By the time they were finished, Tess wanted nothing more than to curl up on the blanket and doze in the sun.

'Barney wants to explore,' Ty announced.

'Of course he does,' Tess said, suppressing a grin, a sigh and an eye-roll all in one movement. She glanced at Krissie.

'Fluffy wants to sleep.' She sighed.

Lucky Fluffy.

'Right, well, we'll take our picnic things back to the car and put Fluffy in her cage to sleep.' Tess had thankfully had the foresight to pack the cage and some newspaper. She left the rear door of the car up and wound down all the windows. 'Okay, which way does Barney want to go?'

They walked beside the river. With the children and puppy racing off in front of her, leaving her momentarily chatter free, Tess was at leisure to enjoy the peace. After only five minutes of walking, they rounded a bend and a low sandstone and wrought-iron wall brought them up short.

Krissie turned back to her. 'What is it?'

Tess glanced over the fence. It was so overgrown it took her a moment to make out what it was. When she did her stomach gave a queer little jerk. 'It's a cemetery,' she said, watching both children carefully.

Neither recoiled, and she let out a breath.

'Can we go in?'

Shielding her eyes against the sun, Tess followed the sandstone wall around until she found what she was looking for. 'The entrance is over there.' She pointed. If they'd driven a little further on they'd have happened upon this spot in the car—it was the very end of the road. Her lips twisted. In more ways than one, she supposed, but she determinedly left the gallows humour behind as she walked through the gate.

'Ty, Krissie.' She gestured to the children. 'There are some rules we need to observe in a cemetery. It's very bad manners to walk on a grave, so please keep to the paths.' And there were some, even if they were terribly overgrown in places. Someone was doing what they could to maintain this little cemetery. 'If you want to look at the headstones walk beside the graves, okay?'

Both children nodded solemnly. 'What about Barney?'

'Puppies are exempt, young man.'

They turned in concert to find an elderly woman, half hidden in the shade of a Kurrajong tree, sitting on a camp chair beside one of the graves. 'I hope we're not disturbing you,' Tess ventured.

'Not at all, lovey.'

Tess moved towards her. 'I'm Tess Laing and this is my nephew and niece—'

'Tyler and Kristina, yes, I've heard about you folk and I'm real pleased you've come to settle in Bellaroo Creek. I'm Edna Fairfield. I meant to make it to your luncheon, but my knees aren't as young as they used to be. My husband, Ted, and I own a pocket of land just back that way.' She nodded back the way Tess and the children had come.

After shy hellos, Ty and Krissie raced off to explore. Tess sat on the grass next to the older woman and Barney settled at her feet to nap. 'I'm afraid we've been trespassing on your land. I'm terribly sorry.'

'You're welcome to wander through our holding whenever you want, lovey.'

They sat in silence for a while. Tess finally gestured. 'Is this a private cemetery?'

'Lord, no, it's the Bellaroo Creek cemetery, but folks these days prefer to scatter the ashes of their loved ones on the land. Hardly anyone comes here any more.'

'But you do?'

'My dear mother and father are buried just over there.' She pointed to a nearby grave. 'And this here—' she touched the edge of the grave she sat beside '—is where we buried my darling boy, Jack. He was only a tiny tot—eighteen months—when croup took him.'

Tess read the dates on the headstone and a lump lodged in her throat. Edna had been coming here for sixty years to sit by her beloved baby son. 'Oh, Mrs Fairfield,' she whispered. 'I'm so sorry for your loss.'

'Don't you go wasting your sympathy on me, young Tess. Ted and me, we raised three healthy children and sent them out into the world—good strong folk we're proud of. Into every life there comes some sorrow.' She might be old but her eyes hadn't faded and they glanced shrewdly at Tess now.

'I understand there's been some recent sorrow in your lives too.'

She nodded. Into every life... She glanced at Ty and Krissie, carefully walking around the graves. 'I'm thinking, though, that moving out here means we can start focusing on good things again.'

Please, God.

'I don't doubt that for a moment.'

She couldn't help smiling at Edna's no-nonsense country briskness.

'But, lovey—' Edna sighed after a moment '—I can't help wondering who'll come here and tend my Jack's grave when Ted and I are gone.' She shook her head. 'It's a silly thing to worry about, I know, but it doesn't stop me from thinking about it.'

'I don't think it's silly.'

She didn't think it was the slightest bit silly. She went to say more but suddenly found Ty and Krissie standing in front of her. Holding hands, no less! 'Everything okay, poppets?'

'Can we bury Mummy here?' Krissie asked without preamble.

Whoa!

Okay.

Um...

She glanced at Edna. 'Is it still possible to arrange a plot here?'

'I expect so, lovey. Lorraine Pritchard would be

the person to ask. She's the president of the Residents Committee.'

'That's Cam's mum,' Ty said to Edna. 'He's our friend.'

'He lives right next door,' Krissie added.

'He's a good young man,' Edna agreed. 'He helps Ted out every now and again. Means we can still manage to keep a few head of cattle on our land.'

He did? Tess stared at Edna. What would she and Ted do when Cam left?

Cam's farm ute was parked out the front when they arrived back home. Tess parked beside it and tried to school her wayward heart back into its normal pace and rhythm instead of a ridiculous speeded-up staccato.

'Can we play on the computer?'

She eyed her nephew and her heart expanded. Two months ago he'd been listless with no enthusiasm for any kind of play. Understandable given the circumstances, but now it seemed the world held a whole list of endless possibilities.

She climbed out of the car and crossed her fingers, prayed the worst was behind them now. 'As long as you promise to let Krissie have her turn too.'

He nodded.

'Okay, go on, then.'

He was about to race off, Krissie at his heels,

when Cam came around the side of the house. 'Hey, Cam.' He waved.

'Hey, kids.'

Krissie flung her arms around Cam's middle and hugged him. Tess couldn't prevent a squirm of envy.

'We found the bestest cemetery,' she announced, releasing him. 'You wanna come play on the computer?'

He blinked. 'Um… Maybe some other time.' He ruffled her hair. 'I have to chat to your aunt about some stuff.'

Krissie ran off and Cam turned to her with a frown. 'What's so hot about a cemetery?'

'They want to inter their mother's ashes there.'

He pushed the brim of his hat back to stare at her. She nodded. 'I know. It took me off guard too. It's all kind of serious, huh?' She twisted her hands together. Once they interred Sarah's remains in the Bellaroo Creek cemetery, there'd be no going back. For good or for ill, Bellaroo Creek would become their home. For good.

'Are you okay with that?'

'Sure.' As long as Bellaroo Creek flourished. As long as the primary school remained open. As long…

She kicked herself into action. Standing still for too long allowed doubts to bombard her. And what was the use in those? Striding around the car, she retrieved Fluffy and the cage.

'So what's wrong?'

She sent him a swift glance. 'Who says anything's wrong?'

'I do. Your eyes are darker than normal and you have a tiny furrow here.' He touched a spot on her forehead, before taking the cage from her.

She folded her arms. How could this man be so attuned to her and yet be so far out of reach? She clamped her lips shut. He *was* out of reach. *That* was the pertinent fact. Everything else was just… wishful thinking.

'Tess?'

She turned away, swallowing back a sigh, and led the way down the side of the house. 'They want to inter their mother's remains in Bellaroo Creek's cemetery, but they've made no mention of their father.'

She plonked herself down on the garden bench and watched Cam as he placed Fluffy into her mansion of a coop. He was a joy to watch. He might be big, but he didn't lumber about like a bear. He moved with the grace of a big cat.

She forced her gaze away, only turning back when he took a seat beside her. 'And that's a problem?'

She thought about it. 'I don't know. Potentially, I guess. We had Sarah and Bruce cremated, but I had no idea what to do with the ashes. A counsellor suggested I let the children be part of the decision-making process, but they were appalled at the thought of scattering the ashes. So…'

'So you brought them with you.'

'They were very insistent that their mother should come with us.'

'But their father?'

'Not a brass razoo.' She shook her head. 'And I couldn't very well leave him behind, could I?'

'I guess not.' He squinted up at the sky. 'I expect they'll need closure at some point.'

'Lord, I hope so.' She grinned at him. 'Because I'm not sure I want Bruce living on the top of my wardrobe for the next twenty years.'

He laughed as she'd meant him to, but he leaned towards her, and that suddenly seemed dangerous. 'And, yet, why do I get the feeling that if that's how long Krissie and Ty need, then that's exactly where Bruce will stay?'

He smelled like cut grass, dirt and fresh air. It hit her that he smelled like Bellaroo Creek. When he went to Africa, he'd be taking a little bit of Bellaroo Creek with him. The thought should've made her smile.

'I met Edna Fairfield.'

He leaned back. 'Keeping Jack company?'

'Uh-huh.'

She eyed him for a moment. He rolled his shoulders. 'What?'

'She has a very high opinion of you.'

'I have a high opinion of her and Ted.'

'They'll miss you if you leave.'

'When, Tess. *When* I leave.'

She shook herself. 'That's what I meant.'

He had exciting, not to mention important, work to look forward to in Africa. He had the promise of adventure before him, the once-in-a-lifetime experience of immersing himself in another culture and sharing his knowledge, and helping make the world a better place. She couldn't begrudge him his dream, but...

She pulled in a breath. 'I liked her a lot. I don't know much about cattle, but...but could you teach me what to do so I can help them out?'

'Nope.'

She gaped at him.

'Lord, Tess, you think I'm just going to abandon them?'

'Well, aren't you?' He was abandoning all of Bellaroo Creek, wasn't he?

'I've told Fraser to keep an eye on things out there, to help wherever needed.'

His station manager? 'It won't be the same, you know?'

'That can't be helped.'

She supposed he was right.

'If you really want to help Edna out, you'll drop out there when her fruit trees are full and pick the fruit for her…and ask her to teach you how to bottle it, and how to make jam. She'd love that.'

'Excellent.' She'd have to find out when the trees came into fruit. Oh, and she'd better find out what kind of fruit trees they were too.

'Plum and mulberry. And you'll be looking at about November.'

The man could read minds.

'And I also think you should come to judo lessons.'

His sudden change of topic threw her like an unexpected rhythm or an atonal jazz riff. 'You mean… participate? Be one of your students?'

'What would it hurt to learn a few self-defence tactics?'

Nothing, she supposed, but she'd never precisely been the sporty type.

'And you're going to be there anyway, bringing Ty and Krissie to the class. So, why not?'

She saw it then, what it was he was trying to do. 'You think Ty and Krissie will feel safer if I know how to defend myself.' Her heart thumped and her hands clenched.

'I think it's a good idea for every woman to know how to defend herself.'

She chewed her bottom lip.

'Come on, Tess, I'm not talking about grating carrots here.'

He was right. 'It's an excellent suggestion.'

'Good.'

'Now what can I do for you?'

He blinked. And for a moment she could've sworn the colour heightened on his cheekbones. Her heart leapt into her throat and it was all she could do not to cough and choke and make a fool of herself. 'I mean,' she rasped out, gazing everywhere except at him, 'I expect there's a reason you dropped by this afternoon, other than to bully me into taking your judo class?'

He leapt off the bench and strode several feet away. 'I wanted to find out what you had in mind for a vegetable garden,' he said, his back to her, and she knew he felt the same heat, the same urgency, that she did. 'I am getting forty prime hectares practically scot-free, after all. I mean to keep my word, Tess. Chicken coop—tick. Puppy—tick. Vegetable garden—still pending.'

'You didn't just build a chicken coop. You built a chicken palace!' As far as she was concerned, he'd well and truly paid off any debt he'd owed.

He turned and squinted into the sun. 'Are you after a, um, vegetable patch on the same sort of scale?'

She laughed at the expression on his face, though she didn't doubt for a moment that if she wanted it he'd do his best to make it a reality. 'Truly, Cameron, I just want a home for all of these.' She gestured to the ragged array of donated pots and planters. 'And whatever else you think might be a good idea to plant.'

'I was sorting through them when you pulled up. You've a nice variety there.'

'The town's generosity knows no bounds.'

'They want you to stay.'

And she wanted to stay. She had to make this move work. She had to. Her smile faded when she recalled the expression on Edna's face when she'd wondered aloud about who would tend Jack's grave when she was gone. A shiver of unease threaded through her.

'You're not having second thoughts, are you?' he rapped out.

'No!'

'But?'

She swallowed. 'But it didn't hit me until today how tenuous the town's survival is. And I've thrown my lot—and Tyler and Krissie's—in with the town's.' What if the school closed? What if the town did die a slow death? What would they do? It would mean more upheaval and that would be her fault.

'Tess.'

She glanced up.

'Nobody can foresee the future. All you can do is make the here and now meaningful.'

Right. She knew he was right.

'And work with the Save-Our-Town committee to attract even more new blood to the area. Okay?'

She drew in a breath and nodded.

He smiled. 'Now are you going to help me measure out this garden bed or what?'

'Aye-aye, sir.' She clicked her heels together. 'Right after I ring your mother. Apparently she's the one I should talk to about organising a plot at the cemetery.'

He dug his phone out of his pocket and tossed it to her. 'She's on speed dial.' Pulling a tape measure from his hip pocket, he moved away to give her a measure of privacy.

She brought up his list of saved numbers. Lorraine's number was the second on the list.

The first was Lance's.

All you can do is make the here and now meaningful.

She stared at Cameron's back as she placed her call.

CHAPTER SEVEN

LORRAINE ORGANISED A working bee at the cemetery with all the speed and efficiency of a conductor's flourish. 'We can't hold a memorial service there with it looking the way it is! It's beyond time we tidied it up.'

Which was why Tess and the kids found themselves getting ready to return to the cemetery the following Saturday. Tess finally managed to convince Krissie that Fluffy would be much happier staying behind in her chicken mansion rather than attending a busy, noisy working bee. When she rose and turned she found Cam standing directly behind her and her skin flared and her stomach tumbled and a bubble of something light and airy rose within her.

Her heart fluttered up into her throat. She swallowed it back down into her chest and tried to pop the bubble with silent verbal thrusts. *He'll be gone soon.* But her brain refused to cooperate. It was too busy revelling in the undiluted masculinity on display. In low-slung jeans, soft with wear, and a faded cotton twill work shirt—with buttons…buttons that could be undone—he made her fingers itch to run all over him in the same way they did whenever she was near a piano.

She took a step back. 'Hello, Cameron.'

He blinked and that was when she realised he'd been staring at her as intently as she'd been staring at him. Her skin flared hotter. They both glanced away.

'Are you coming with us to the working bee?' Krissie asked.

'Working bee?'

He glanced at Tess. She frowned. Hadn't Lorraine spoken to him? *None of your business.* She cleared her throat and folded her arms. 'The town's organised a clean-up of the cemetery. We're just about to head out there now.'

'I didn't hear about it.'

She unfolded her arms. Well, why not? It— *None of your business.* She folded her arms again.

'You have to come,' Ty said. 'It won't be the same if you're not there.'

That was one way of putting it.

Cam smoothed a hand down his jaw. 'The thing is, buddy, I was going to start on your vegetable garden today.'

'But we want to help you do that, don't we, Auntie Tess?'

'We do.'

'And the working bee is for our mummy.' Krissie slid her hand into Cam's. 'Please…you have to come.'

Tess had to choke back a laugh. Talk about emotional blackmail! She clapped her hands briskly. 'Okay, kids, grab your hats and, Ty, make sure you bring Barney's lead.'

The kids raced off.

Cam stared at her. She sucked her bottom lip into her mouth. He followed the action and his eyes darkened. She released it again, her pulse pounding in her throat. She wheeled away to stare blindly at the backyard. 'I don't feel right about you working here without us being around to help. I want to learn.'

'It'll mostly be brute work today.'

'Nevertheless.'

There was a pause. 'Is that a roundabout way of saying you'd like me to come to the cemetery instead?'

'I'd love you to come.' And she meant it. She really wanted him to be part of the working bee, but she wasn't quite sure what that meant. Except she needed to be careful. *Very* careful.

She needed to fight her fascination for this man, or it would all end in tears. If they were only her tears that wouldn't matter, but… She glanced towards the house. 'I think it's only fair to warn you that I expect your mother, Lance and Fiona will all be there today.'

Again there was a long pause. 'You think I'm afraid to come face-to-face with them?'

He stole all that I most cherished.

'I think you've been doing your best to avoid them.' A part of her didn't blame him. She wouldn't want to come face-to-face with the person she loved more than life itself on a daily basis and know they'd chosen someone else. And not just any anonymous *someone else* either, but a sibling. It'd be like ripping a scab off a wound again and again.

She could understand why he wanted to leave Bellaroo Creek. She could even see why he might need to. She couldn't see that cutting himself off from the entire community in the meantime was the thing to do, though. He hadn't done anything to be ashamed of.

'You know—' she planted her hands on her hips '—I think you've made it awfully easy for Lance and Fiona. It wouldn't hurt them to have to see you on a regular basis and feel awkward and ashamed about what they've done.'

He laughed. It surprised her. 'It's nice to have you in my corner, Tess.'

Was that what she was? *You want to be a whole lot more than just in his corner.* She shook the thought off, refused to follow it, tried to focus on the conversation. 'That's your problem with your mother, isn't it? You feel she's not on your side.'

'She's not,' he said bluntly. 'She's always favoured

Lance. And, no, that's not jealous sibling rivalry talking, Tess, but...'

Her heart stilled at the expression on his face. 'But?'

'I realised something when we were up at the school the other day. When my mother left my father, he withdrew into himself. He still managed the farm but he had no social life. He let all his friendships slip; he let his position in the community go. When he died he'd closed himself off so completely that the only person left to mourn him was me.'

She pressed a hand to her chest. 'Oh, Cameron, I'm so sorry.' What a terrible story. And what a sad household for a boy to grow up in. No wonder—

'But I have no intention of following his lead.'

She stared at him for a long moment. 'That's one of the reasons you're going overseas.'

'I might never have a wife and children, but it doesn't mean I can't find meaning in something I'm passionate about. It doesn't mean I can't have adventures and contribute to the world.'

Helping to feed the world would be a huge contribution. Africa would be an amazing adventure. He'd experience the most awe-inspiring things and eventually his heart would heal. Eventually.

'But in the meantime, it's time to stop holing up like a hermit.'

She lifted her chin. 'I think that's an excellent plan.'

He stared at her and then pursed his lips. 'But?'

This is none of your business. She lifted a shoulder. 'Just because things didn't work out with Fiona doesn't mean you'll never fall in love again.'

He shook his head. 'I saw what love did to my father.' His eyes grew grim, dark…shadowed. 'No, thanks, once was enough. I'm not diving into that particular hellhole again. I'll find satisfaction elsewhere.'

She grimaced. Feeding the world was all well and good, but an abstract concept couldn't give you a big fat hug when you needed it. She opened her mouth but he held up a hand. 'Leave it now, Tess.'

She moistened her lips and then nodded. He'd make friends on his adventure. They'd look after him. For no reason at all, a hole opened up inside her.

'You know,' she started, turning back towards the house, 'I used to be really good at minding my own business.'

One side of his mouth hooked up. 'I don't believe that for a moment.'

The thing was, it was true. She'd been too caught up in her music to notice if anyone had been feeling down or worried. How selfish she'd been! She'd been too self-absorbed to involve herself in other people's problems, in other people's lives. In a way, she'd cut herself off as comprehensively as Cam had.

Her chest burned. Giving up music had been a good thing.

But that bubble of half-happiness half-excitement that had been floating around inside her ever since she'd turned and seen Cameron finally popped.

'Would you like to come with us, Cam?'

'I'll meet you at the cemetery. I'll run back home and collect a few tools first.'

She waved him off as Ty and Krissie piled into the car. She pushed her shoulder back and drew in a breath. A big one. These kids were worth every sacrifice she'd have to make. She'd choose them over music any day of the week—even when they were running her ragged. She'd choose them over a man.

Yes. She slid behind the steering wheel and nodded. This was the life they were meant to be living. *I won't let you down, Sarah.*

Lorraine set the men to work with lawnmowers and whipper-snippers clearing the scrub from around the fence line and mowing the paths. The women and children she set to work clearing weeds from around the graves and scrubbing headstones clean of moss and lichen. Having never been a part of a working bee before, Tess enjoyed the sense of camaraderie with the dozen or so other workers.

As expected, the handful of children eventually took off to play in the neighbouring paddock—eight children, three dogs and two soccer balls. One of the older women kept an eye on them. 'Don't worry yourself,' she'd said to Tess when Tess had wandered over to check on them for the third time. 'We know out here that at least one person needs to keep an eye on the children to avert potential accidents. And it's a treat for me to sit in the sun like this and listen to the littlies.'

With her fears eased, she'd returned to work pulling weeds from around a grave.

Lorraine came up, touched her arm. 'Tess, I want to thank you for convincing Cameron to come along.'

Tess sat back on her heels. 'I had nothing to do with it. I was only surprised he didn't know about it.'

The older woman's hand fluttered about her throat. She glanced away.

'When the children told him, though, he was more than happy to lend a hand.'

Lorraine turned back with an overbright smile. 'All I can say is that it's lovely to see him here.'

Tess met the other woman's gaze. 'Then you might want to tell him that some time.'

She blinked. 'You think he'd…' She swallowed. 'It's his birthday next Sunday, you know? It's one of those birthdays that ends in a zero. Maybe I…'

Tess didn't want to appear too interested. She went back to pulling weeds. 'Are you planning anything special?' Would she like Tess's help?

'Oh, no, I don't think so. I don't think he'd welcome that.'

The older woman's sigh touched her heart. The secateurs suddenly felt heavy in her hands. What would she do if Ty and Krissie were ever at sixes and sevens the way Cam and Lance were? She suppressed a shudder. She'd do everything in her power to make sure that never happened. If it did, she'd do everything in her power to fix it.

But what if that wasn't enough?

'Listen to me rambling on! Time to get back to work.'

Lorraine moved away to oversee more job delegation. Tess glanced around until she found Cam's broad capable bulk, whipper-snipper in hand, cutting a swathe through the long grass on the other side of the cemetery. He looked at ease, comfortable, in his element, and Tess followed his lead, giving herself up to working in the fresh air beneath an autumn sun that wasn't too fierce.

'Hello, I'm Fiona. We met briefly at the luncheon.'

Tess blinked to find the flawless blonde working on the other side of the grave. She suddenly found herself battling the desire to reach out and slap the other woman or to just get up and walk away.

Whoa!

She rocked back on her heels. 'I remember,' she managed, but something in her tone made the other woman flush.

Be nice! 'Gorgeous day for it, isn't it?'

'Yes.' Fiona didn't immediately set back to work, but stared at a point beyond Tess's right shoulder. 'Cam is looking well.'

Ah… 'Well? Gorgeous more like.' She turned to look too. 'That man is a sight for sore eyes.'

When she turned back she found Fiona staring at her. 'Are you and Cam—?' She broke off. 'Sorry, that's none of my business.'

Tess went back to weeding. She had no intention of satisfying Fiona's curiosity.

'Look, Tess.' Fiona set her clippers down. 'What I really want to know is if he's doing as well as he looks.'

Tess glanced up. 'Why don't you ask him some time? I understand you used to be close.'

The flawless skin suddenly flushed pink. 'Oh! You think I'm a right piece of work, don't you?' She sat with a thump on the side of the grave—a cement rectangle with an angel atop the headstone. Tess kept her mouth very firmly shut. 'I never meant for all this to happen. I never meant to fall in love with Lance and cause a rift between the brothers.'

And yet she had. And from what Tess could see, Fiona wasn't doing anything about it—wasn't trying to bridge gaps or make amends.

'I know Cam is the better man.'

That had Tess's head swinging around.

'The thing is, you see, he never really needed me.

He's so strong and honourable and…self-sufficient. I can't complain about the way he treated me—he treated me like a queen—and yet… I never felt I'd made much of an impact on him.'

How wrong Fiona had been! She opened her mouth and then snapped it shut again. She had no intention of betraying Cam's confidence.

'But with Lance…'

Fiona turned to glance at Lance and her whole face lit up. Tess's stomach clenched.

'Lance needs me.' She turned back to Tess, her face earnest. 'I feel I can help make him a better man. I don't expect you to understand because you're strong, like Cam.'

Her, strong? That was laughable.

'Taking on your niece and nephew like you have proves that,' Fiona continued. 'But I'm the kind of person who needs to be needed. And that's why I'm with Lance instead of Cam.'

Couldn't she have found a different man who needed her instead of Cam's brother?

A bustle at the front gates interrupted them. 'It's the CWA with lunch,' Fiona explained, rising. 'I'll go lend them a hand.'

'You do that,' Tess muttered under her breath, pulling out a weed with a vicious tug. No doubt the CWA *needed* her. Man, what a flake! What on earth had Cam seen in her?

Other than her flawless skin.

And her perky blonde ponytail.

Oh, and her model-like figure.

She sat back on her heels scowling at the grave, but after a moment she started to laugh. Oh, did she have the green-eyed monster bad or what? Fiona was probably a perfectly nice woman. And to give her credit, she did seem genuinely sorry for hurting Cam and creating a rift between him and Lance.

Though, from what Cam had said, that rift had been widening well before Fiona had come onto the scene.

Mind your own business.

As for the jealousy, she had no right to that. No right whatsoever.

Cam was more than ready for lunch when it was announced. Breakfast seemed like hours ago and he expected they'd all worked up healthy appetites. He joined the throng around the CWA tables and started loading up a paper plate with sandwiches and party pies.

'Hello, Cam, would you like a mug of tea?'

Fiona. He waited for his gut to clench. It did. A fraction. Not as much as he expected, though.

'Thanks.' He nodded.

'Are you well?'

She was obviously trying to make an effort.

'Never better.' He went to ask her how she was, but his arm was suddenly tugged.

'Cam,' Ty asked, 'can I feed Barney a party pie?'

'Sure you can, buddy. Just make sure it's cooled down first, okay?'

And then he found he'd wandered away from the table and he hadn't made the polite enquiry of Fiona after all. With a shrug, he set off for a spot in the shade of a Kurrajong tree.

'Hey, Tess.' Lance called out from his spot in the sun on the other side of the gated entrance from Cam. 'Why don't you join us?'

Cam's gut clenched up tighter than a newly sprung barbed-wire fence. With his back stiff and rigid, he kept moving towards the Kurrajong tree.

'No, thanks,' Tess called back. 'I prefer the view over here.' And then she was sitting beside him on the newly clipped grass and gesturing at the scene spread in front of them. 'It's really starting to take shape, isn't it?'

The woman stole his breath.

'This working-bee idea is really something.'

He glanced around at the clumps of people settling down to have their lunch and his throat tightened. He'd honestly thought, once, that he could make his simple dream come true in this community. Days like today brought the disappointment home to him afresh. And yet...

He couldn't deny it'd been invigorating working in the sun, side by side with people he'd known his entire life. He glanced at Tess—and some he'd known for less than a month.

'Yeah, I guess it is,' he finally agreed. And if she noticed the strain in his voice, she didn't mention it.

I prefer the view over here.

He found himself starting to grin.

'I think this will be the perfect spot to bury Sarah.' She shrugged when he glanced at her. 'Well, to inter her ashes or whatever it's called. You know what I mean. It's a nice spot for a final resting place.'

He supposed she was right.

'What did you do with your father's remains, Cameron?'

'I scattered his ashes on Kurrajong Station. It's what he wanted.'

She nodded and bit into a sandwich. 'That's nice too.'

What about her parents? Were they still living? 'Will your parents come to the memorial service?'

'I doubt it.'

She lowered her sandwich to her plate and he immediately regretted asking the question. 'Forget I asked,' he ordered. 'It's none of my business.'

She shot him a look that made him laugh, and then she shrugged. 'I don't mind. It's kind of funny coming to a place like Bellaroo Creek. You've all known each other so long that you know each other's histories.'

She turned those big brown eyes to him and he

had to swallow. He shifted and covered his lap with his plate, and hoped she didn't notice how tightly he gritted his teeth.

'It's nice,' she finally finished.

'You're fitting in brilliantly.'

She flashed him a smile. 'I'm not feeling insecure, but thank you. I know it'll take time, but so far it's going better than I'd hoped.'

That was okay, then.

'My parents are…distant,' she said, picking her sandwich up again. 'Sarah and I actually came from quite a privileged background, but to be honest I'm not really sure why my parents had children. We were raised by nannies.'

The sweet vulnerable curve of her mouth turned down and her slender shoulders drooped for a moment, and an ugly darkness welled in his gut.

'So, to be honest with you, I don't really know them. Obviously they came to Sarah and Bruce's actual funeral.'

But he could see now that they'd provided Tess with no support whatsoever.

'And I very much doubt they'll ever visit us out here at Bellaroo Creek. They've been living in America these last few years.'

He shifted. 'Privileged, you say?'

She nodded.

'So, you could've organised nannies for Ty and Krissie and kept your career?'

'It's what my parents wanted me to do.'

He saw now that Tess had too much compassion and natural sympathy, too much integrity to have abandoned her niece and nephew.

She rolled her eyes. 'Apparently a daughter who's a concert pianist and fêted classical guitarist has more cachet than one who is merely a mother and housekeeper.'

They should be proud of her and all she'd taken on!

'I couldn't let Sarah down,' she said softly.

He reached out and briefly clasped her hand. 'She'd be proud of you, Tess.'

'I hope so,' she whispered, her eyes suspiciously bright. She blinked and then resumed eating. 'We always promised each other that if we ever had children we'd be hands-on parents—the opposite of our own.'

He understood that perfectly. He couldn't imagine having a child and then farming it out for other people to look after. Even the folk around here who sent their kids to boarding school couldn't wait for end of term time.

'She left me a letter, you know?'

'Sarah?'

She nodded.

'She knew something was going to happen to her?'

'I think after Bruce's accident it really hit home

to her how life can change in an instant. She said she wouldn't offend me by asking me to raise Ty and Krissie as if they were my own—she knew I would. She told me all the good things I had to offer them. And then she told me about the life insurance policy she'd organised so we'd never have to worry about money.'

'She wanted to be prepared,' he murmured. In case life ever played her another nasty trick. She'd been smart.

'Which is why you should get married and have kids, Cam. 'Cause, the way things currently stand, if anything happens to you Lance will probably inherit Kurrajong Station, and we can't have that.'

He stared, and then he threw his head back and laughed. 'You never give up, do you?'

'Nope.'

He shook his head. 'Sarah sounds like a hell of a woman, Tess.'

'She was.' Her eyes turned misty and faraway and he knew she no longer saw the cemetery and this golden autumn day. 'She was four years older and became a bit of a surrogate mother to me.'

'And you hero-worshipped her, right?' She'd had the kind of relationship with Sarah he'd hungered to have with Lance. He promptly lost his appetite.

Tess laughed. He loved the sound. 'I expect I plagued her half to death. But I remember...'

She leaned forward, her eyes dreamy and distant

again. Thirst snaked through him and the longer he gazed at her, the thirstier he became, but he couldn't tear his eyes away. 'What do you remember?'

'Music was my passion.' She sat back. 'No, it was more than that. It drove me, rode me...obsessed me. I would practise for hours and hours, driven to get a piece just right. I'd stay up into the wee small hours, practising and playing and practising more and more. And Sarah would sit up with me, and when I was about to drop with exhaustion she'd put me to bed.'

His heart started to ache. Ty and Krissie had lost their mother, and that was a terrible thing. But Tess had lost a sister—a much-loved sister—and who had held her in their arms and let her cry out her grief?

Certainly not her parents.

Tears swam in her eyes. 'I miss her so much.'

He reached out to touch her cheek, but suddenly a little dynamo in the shape of Krissie burst up between them. Her bottom lip wobbled as she stared at Tess. 'Why are you crying?'

Tess held her arms open and Krissie threw herself into them. His heart clenched when Tess lifted her face to the sun and dragged in a breath to steady herself.

So strong!

'I was just telling Cam about your mum and I got to missing her.'

'I miss her too,' Krissie whispered.

'I know, chickadee.'

Krissie snuggled closer. 'Tell me a story about when you and Mummy were kids like Ty and me. Were you ever naughty?'

'Never!'

Tess feigned shock and Krissie giggled.

'Except—' she winked '—this one time when we were in high school. We both really, *really* wanted to see this movie—*Charlie's Angels*—and we actually snuck out of school early to go and watch it.'

Krissie covered her mouth with both her hands, her eyes wide.

'What's more, we bought the biggest popcorn we could find and the biggest cola you ever did see.'

'Did you get caught?' Krissie breathed.

'No, but we got the biggest tummy aches, which served us right for being such gluttons!'

Tess tickled Krissie until she squealed with delight and then ran back off to find what the other children were doing.

Cam wanted to hug Tess the way she'd hugged Krissie. He wanted to tickle her until she felt better too.

His lips twisted. Who was he trying to kid? He wanted to kiss her until neither one of them could think straight. But that wouldn't make her feel better, not in the long term.

He blinked to find her eyeing him as hungrily as he did her. His skin tightened, but he ignored it.

He had to tread carefully around this woman. She'd taken on a lot. She'd sacrificed a lot, and it would be cruel and thoughtless of him to make her life harder. She didn't deserve that.

She deserved to grow roots and be surrounded by a community that would look out for her. She deserved to be loved by a man who could give her security and a loving family. She deserved a man who meant to stay in Bellaroo Creek.

He crushed his plate into a ball. He wasn't any of those things.

But…

There was one more thing she deserved. 'Tess?'

'Hmm?'

'I think you're making a big mistake.'

She swung to him, brown eyes wide and alert. 'About?'

'Giving up your music.'

Her face closed up. 'I haven't given it up. I'm giving music lessons for the school, aren't I? Ty, Krissie and I sing all the time—I'm teaching them to harmonise. As for being on stage—'

'I'm not talking about being on stage. Tess, when was the last time you played the piano or picked up a guitar?'

She flinched. 'What's that got to do with anything?'

'I think it has everything to do with it.'

'You don't know what you're talking about.'

Every instinct he had told him he was right. Sacrificing something that was such a part of who she was would damage her in a fundamental way. Maybe not this year or the next, but eventually. 'Do you think Sarah would approve of you punishing yourself like this?'

Tess went to leap up, but he grabbed her arm. 'I'm not going to let this lie, Tess. I'm going to get to the bottom of it.'

She subsided back to the ground beside him. 'And what do you think you're going to find when you do? Do you think it's going to be pretty or something you can fix? Because it's not pretty and it can't be fixed. So as far as I'm concerned talking about it is pointless.'

'I mightn't be able to fix it, Tess, but bottling it up won't help either.'

She had to look away then because his eyes told her he only wanted her to be happy. And she knew his questions came from a good place, not a bad one.

'Tess?'

And he wouldn't leave it alone; she knew that too. If he knew the truth then he'd see that she was right. Even if it did change his opinion of her for the worse.

'Sarah asked me to come home at the beginning of December.' She stared at her hands. 'But I had a whole series of concerts lined up and I put her off for a month.'

A whole month!

'Later, when I did get home…' When it was too late. 'I found out Sarah had been trying to set up a second residence and was in the process of moving the children there.'

She'd wanted Tess to come home and help her. But Tess, in her selfishness and self-absorption, had put Sarah off for a whole month. Who knew what they could've accomplished together in a month, what changes they could've made…what disasters they could've averted. Instead of making a difference in her sister's life, she'd chosen to shine on stage instead.

She straightened. But she wouldn't let Sarah down again. She'd look after Ty and Krissie and give them all the love she had, give them the absolute best lives she could. It wouldn't be enough. It would never be enough. But it was something.

'Hey!'

She blinked at the hard command in Cam's voice.

'Did she tell you why she wanted you to come home?'

'No, but—'

'Then you have nothing to beat yourself up about.'

He was wrong about that. 'She asked so little of me over the years.' *She should've come home.*

'She should've been straight with you. Nothing that happened to Bruce and Sarah was of your making.'

'No, but—'

'And whipping yourself into a frenzy of guilt is ludicrous. You didn't cause Bruce's accident. You weren't driving the car that left the road and hit the tree. Hell, Tess, you're giving these kids a great life. You should be proud of yourself.'

Proud of herself for not being there when Sarah had needed her? Never!

'Depriving yourself of your music—'

She leaned towards him. 'When I chose my music over Sarah, music let me down. I let me down. But, worse, I let Sarah down.' She shook her head. 'I'm not risking that again.'

'Tess, I think Sarah would weep in her grave if she knew all you'd given up.'

Tears clogged her throat. This time when she leapt up, he let her go. 'My life has a different focus now and I'm pleased about that.' *She was!* She pointed behind her. 'I'll go help clear the food away.'

Tess had been working steadily for an hour when Lance stormed up. 'You have no right upsetting Fi!'

She stared up at him. 'Lower your voice,' she snapped. 'You upset my kids again and I will have your guts for garters, got it?'

His mouth opened and closed. He dropped down to sit on the side of the grave she was working on. 'I, uh…I didn't mean to appear so…'

She quirked an eyebrow. 'Aggressive?'

He raked a hand through his pretty blond hair.

'I've never thought of myself as scary to kids before,' he muttered.

'Then maybe you should stop puffing your chest out and beating it in that ridiculous fashion, and learn some manners.'

She swore his jaw dropped to the ground at his feet. She didn't doubt for a single moment that the women in his life mollycoddled him, and she had no intention of joining their ranks.

Still…

She rose, planting her hands on her hips. 'And I didn't upset Fiona. I suspect she upset herself. I believe it's called a guilty conscience.'

He turned beet-red and glanced away. Interesting. Maybe he wasn't immune to a guilty conscience either.

'Still, at least it appears you really do love her.'

He swung back. 'Of course I love her.' He gazed to where Fiona worked and his face took on a goofy expression. 'I mean, she's the best girl in the world.' He glanced back at her, the blue of his eyes suddenly bleak. 'I didn't mean to…'

She waited but he didn't go on. 'You're wrong about Cam too. He's not trying to ruin you. I doubt he'd ever stoop to something so petty.'

He squinted down at the ground. 'Cam never was petty. But after what I did, who could blame him for wanting his revenge?'

She let the silence speak for her.

He rose with a sick kind of pallor. 'I wish...'

She ran out of patience with him then. 'For God's sake, stop thinking about yourself for once! Have you ever considered actually apologising to Cameron for your appalling behaviour?'

His eyes started from his head. 'Are you joking? He wouldn't listen. I expect he'd deck me!'

'Then you're a stupider man than I thought.' With that, she turned away sick to her stomach. Cam deserved so much more than what any of his family had given him.

It's nice to have you in my corner.

She set her shoulders. Cam mightn't be here for much longer, but for as long as he was in Bellaroo Creek she had every intention of remaining in his corner.

CHAPTER EIGHT

'Shouldn't we buy Cam a present if it's his birth-day?'

Tess glanced at Ty. 'I think you and Krissie should make him a birthday card. I bought cardboard, glitter pens and stickers.' She'd lugged them all the way from Sydney sure they'd find a use for them, and she set them on the kitchen table now. 'Plus, we are making him the best cake in the world.'

'With cream and jam in the middle and sprinkles on top?' Krissie double-checked.

'That's right, chickadee.'

'And I'm going to take my pin-the-tail on the don-key game,' she added. 'I think Cam will love play-ing that.'

'I'm sure you're right.'

'I know!' Ty's face lit up. 'I can write him a story. We're writing stories at school and Mrs Bennet said I was good at them.'

'Cam would love a story,' Tess agreed. 'And you

can make a proper cover for it out of the cardboard and draw a picture on it.'

Hopefully book and card building would keep the two of them occupied for the next thirty minutes while she worked out how to cut her sponge in half, fill it with jam and cream, and then ice it.

Krissie suddenly rose from the kitchen table to press herself to Tess's side. 'Mrs Bennet's leaving at the end of the year. She's re…re…'

Tess's heart clenched at the anxiety that threaded through her niece's eyes. How she wished she could shield them from everything that worried or frightened them. 'She's retiring.' Tess's own heart clenched then too. 'Which means you'll have a brand-new teacher next year.' Please, God, because if Bellaroo Creek couldn't attract a new teacher to town, and the school closed…

Her stomach churned, but she made her voice cheerful. 'And we'll have to make sure they feel as welcome to town as we did.'

'And then we won't be the newest people any more,' Ty said.

Krissie bit her lip. 'Do you think we'll like her… or him?'

Ty glanced up at Krissie's 'or him', his eyes wary. It made Tess's heart burn harder. 'I'm sure we will.' She sent them both her biggest smile. Reassured, they returned to their card and story making.

'That's the best cake in the world!' Krissie said

in awe a little while later when Tess stepped away from the cake to admire her handiwork.

'And that's one super-duper card.' Tess picked it up to admire Krissie's handiwork.

'And I'm finished too!'

Ty handed her the book he'd made. He'd stapled the pages between cardboard and had drawn a… um… She'd challenge even Sarah to hazard a guess about that one. 'It looks just like a proper book!'

That was obviously the right response because Ty beamed at her. 'It's a story about a cowboy.'

'Which will be perfect for Cam,' she agreed, glancing again at the cover trying to make out either a cow or a horse or a cowboy.

She clapped her hands. 'Okay, go wash your hands, put on your party clothes and let's go surprise Cam.'

He'd been here yesterday afternoon, building the bed for the vegetable garden. He hadn't let slip for a single moment that he had a birthday today. He'd said he was going to catch up on his bookkeeping.

On a Sunday?

On his birthday?

Oh, no, no. Tess had decided then and there that the least she could do was make him a birthday cake. Somewhere along the line, that had evolved into a full-blown party. Grinning, she went to put on her pink party dress. A party was exactly what they all needed.

* * *

Cameron stilled, cocked his head to one side and then frowned. Someone was knocking on the front door.

Nobody knocked on the front door. Ever. The few people who came out to Kurrajong these days came around the back. Fraser would've tapped on the French doors of Cam's study if he'd needed to discuss anything.

More knocking sounded. He pushed away from his computer with a growl and set off through the dim hush of the house. Since he'd taken a bedroom at the back, he rarely came into this part of the house any more. These big front reception rooms with their picture rails, antiques and high ceilings held the memory of too many shattered dreams. He scowled as he strode through them now. He flung the heavy door open, a bitter reproof burning on his tongue…

A reproof he swallowed at the sight that met his eyes. A sight as colourful as a flock of rosellas and just as cheerful.

'Surprise!' Ty and Krissie yelled, almost in unison, and then they each popped a party popper that covered him in coloured streamers, and for a moment he felt just as colourful—as flamingo-pink and butter-yellow as the girls' party dresses and as purple and blue as Ty's best jeans and shirt.

But then the shadows of the rooms behind touched

the back of his neck with cold fingers, mocking him with the ludicrousness of any colour surviving within their forbidding walls, and he pulled the streamers from his head and shoulders, and a hard ball settled in the pit of his stomach.

'Happy birthday, Cameron.'

Tess's smile almost melted the coldness. 'How on earth…?'

She waggled a finger at him. 'You needn't think you can keep something as important as a birthday a secret.'

As far as he was concerned, it was just another day.

'And we wanted to give you a party, because you're one of our best new friends!'

The smile Krissie sent him did melt the coldness. And while he wished with all his might that they'd turn around and walk back home, he managed to cover his lack of enthusiasm with a smile. 'A party?'

Ty held up a bag. 'We brought jellybeans and crisps!'

'And Auntie Tess made you a cake.'

He glanced at Tess, delectable in her pink dress, but her smile had slipped. She'd sensed his discomfort. 'I hope we haven't caught you at a bad time.'

He blinked. He straightened. She was giving him an out? He could tell them he was really busy, promise to drop over to their place in a couple of hours…

And Tess would turn the children around and walk away, and leave him in peace?

But when he glanced at the kids with their eager shining faces, he didn't have the heart to disappoint them. He could manage a party in this cold, heartless house just this once. It wouldn't kill him. He dragged in a breath and made himself grin. 'A party sounds like just the thing!'

He was rewarded with a smile from Tess that almost knocked him off his feet.

'Your house is amazing,' Ty breathed, glancing around Cam's bulk. He frowned and edged closer to his aunt. 'It's a bit dark.'

He translated that immediately into, *It's a bit scary*. He kept his voice steadily cheerful. 'Well, with only me living here these days I don't use these front rooms much.'

'Auntie Tess was right,' Krissie whispered to her brother. 'We should've gone around the back.'

'But I wanted to see,' he whispered back.

Cam then found himself pushing the door open as wide as he could, beckoning his visitors inside and turning into the reception room to his left and throwing open the curtains as wide as they would go, so the children could take in the room in its entirety, sans shadows. He strode across the corridor and did the same for the other reception room. The children trailed behind him, oohing and ahhing, their eyes wide and mouths agape.

When Tess saw the dark cherrywood baby grand in the second room, she froze. He took the cake from her before she could drop it. He recognised the fear in her eyes, but there was something else there too, fighting for supremacy. She closed her eyes, but not before he saw raw, naked hunger.

With sudden resolution, he turned back to Krissie and Ty. 'It's been a long time since I used this room, but I think it makes the perfect party room, don't you?'

'Yes!'

He set the cake down on a colonial-style hardwood coffee table. He took the bags of party food from Ty and set them there too. 'Then let's get some plates and drinks and then we can really get this party on the road.'

He led them through the formal dining room with its magnificent table-seating for twelve.

Ty gazed at it in awe. 'You must be able to have the biggest parties.'

'Legend has it that my grandparents threw the kind of parties that people spoke about for years.'

There were photo albums showing these rooms filled to bursting with smiling people, dressed in their best. As a boy, he'd pored over those photographs. He'd yearned to be in those photographs, and he'd sworn to bring that kind of gaiety back to Kurrajong House—a dream he'd finally thought within reach when Fiona had agreed to marry him. His hand clenched. How wrong he'd been. He couldn't re-create the gaiety of that bygone era. Not with the kind of family he had.

But he refused to fade away as his father had done.

'Cameron?'

Tess touched his arm. He stared down at her and had to fight the urge to haul her into his arms and kiss her. Falling into her would chase away the ghosts of the past and ease the hurt of shattered dreams, at least for a little while. If he backed her up against the wall, teased her, seduced her...

He could lose himself in her arms and take all he wanted.

And he wanted all right, no doubt about that, but it'd be a despicable thing to do.

She bit her lip—her plump, delectable bottom lip—and her eyes darkened at whatever she saw in his face. The pulse at the base of her throat fluttered. He wanted to press his lips to that spot and—

'The kitchen?' she croaked.

Gritting his teeth, he swung away. 'This way.'

They collected plates, bowls and cans of soda, and headed back to the so-dubbed party room. Cam opened the two front bay windows. A warm breeze filtered through, fanning the lace curtains, a touch of white against the dark wood panelling. While he did that, Tess and the children put out the party food—a big bowl of crisps, smaller bowls of jellybeans and chocolates, a plate of ginger-crisp biscuits, and even a small cheese platter.

He didn't have much of a sweet tooth, but his mouth started to water.

Tess, with her back very firmly to the piano, placed three blue candles on top of the cake and then lit them. She glanced at Krissie and Ty. 'Ready?'

They huddled in around her and at the tops of their voices sang the Happy Birthday song to him, and the longer it went on the wider their grins grew.

'Blow out the candles,' Tess ordered.

He did and they popped more party poppers. Krissie handed him a card she'd made out of glitter and stamps, and Ty handed him a story he'd written about a cowboy, and Cam found himself laughing and eating jellybeans and playing pin the tail on the donkey…and having a party.

He pulled up short when Fraser and Jenny appeared in the doorway a short while later. 'We came to investigate the noise,' Jenny said.

Cam leapt to his feet. 'Come and join us. Tess, Ty and Krissie, this is my station manager, Fraser, and his wife, Jenny, who manages to keep this place clean and running smoothly.' They'd be Tess's nearest neighbours when he left. It would be good for her to know them.

'Lovely to meet you.' Tess beamed at them. 'And you've arrived at the perfect time. We were just about to play pass the parcel.'

Everyone ended up with a snack-sized chocolate except Cam, who won the final prize of a family block of chocolate.

He stared at it—*a family*. He gazed about the room. At the moment they had all the appearance of a family. His heart started to pound, but he pushed the fantasies away. He wouldn't be beguiled by them. Not for a second time. He knew his own strength. He could survive one let-down, but two? He shook his head.

He couldn't deny, though, that for the space of an afternoon Tess and her kids with their laughter and this party had brought a spark of life back into this cold mausoleum of a house.

Krissie slipped a hand inside his. 'Are you having a good party, Cam?'

'The best,' he assured her. 'There's only one more thing that would make it perfect.'

They all swung to him. Tess planted her hands on her hips. 'What could we have possibly forgotten?'

His heart started to thump. She wouldn't thank him for this. At least, not initially, but... He glanced about the room. She'd given him a marvellous memory to take away with him when he left Bellaroo Creek. Instead of seeing his father sitting here in the half-dark, he'd now see Tess in her pink dress and hear the children's laughter.

'Come on, out with it,' she ordered.

He planted his feet. 'I'd like you to play something for me on the piano.'

* * *

Wind rushed in Tess's ears. The room shrank in on her. She collapsed onto a footstool.

No! Cameron couldn't ask this of her. He couldn't. It was too cruel. She'd kept her back firmly to the piano because the lure of it was like a siren song.

She knew he didn't mean to be cruel. He couldn't know about the hole that had opened up in her as big and as dry as the Great Western Desert since she'd packed away her guitar and stopped playing the piano

'I don't play any more,' she whispered, aching to sit at that beautiful piano and to fill her soul with music, but—

She'd turned her back on that life. On that person she'd been.

'I don't have parties,' Cam said, 'but I made an exception today and I don't regret it.' He glanced at the children and then at her again. 'Make an exception, Tess, just for today.'

She glanced at the children then too. The hope in their faces tore at her. Didn't they know that if she'd been a better person—if she'd never played music— their mother might still be alive?

Krissie hopped from one leg to the other, clapping her hands silently, hope filling her eyes—eyes the same shape and colour as Sarah's. Ty came over to where she sat and pressed his hands to either side of her face. 'Please, Auntie Tess? Mummy loved to hear you play.'

Her heart nearly fell out of her chest. It took every ounce of strength she had not to cry. Cam came across and held out a hand to her. She stared at it, swallowed and then reached up and took it, allowed him to help her to her feet and lead her across to the piano.

'What would you like me to play?' she murmured, once seated.

'Whatever you want,' he said, moving to sit across the room from her in an easy chair.

Her hands shook as she played a tentative scale and she had to suck in a breath at the familiarity, at the need growing in her.

Oh, play that one again, Tessie. I love that one. It makes me feel as if I'm flying above the treetops.

Tuning out the doubts, Tess gave herself up to playing one of Sarah's favourite pieces. It filled her up. It made her feel—for a short time—as if she'd found her sister again.

As ever, the music transported her. When she finished she couldn't tell if she'd played it well or not. The stunned faces in front of her told her it'd been good.

Cameron leaned towards her and she imagined she could feel the strength of his regard and his admiration all the way across the room. 'Superb.' And the expression in his eyes made her feel as if she were flying above treetops.

Then she saw a movement by the doorway. Glancing at Cam, she rose and nodded towards his visitors.

Lorraine. Fiona. And Lance.

All the adults rose, but nobody spoke. Finally Jenny cleared her throat. She glanced at Ty and Krissie. 'Would you like to see where Fraser and I live? It's just out the back,' she added to Tess. 'And I can show you the lambs.'

Krissie and Ty leapt to their feet.

'You could come meet the horses too,' Fraser added, winning over one little boy in an instant.

Tess went to start after them, but Jenny touched her arm with a murmured, 'You might like to stay here.'

Tess didn't want to stay. She didn't want to intrude. But she recognised the vulnerability behind the stiff set of Cam's shoulders and the grim line of his mouth. *It's nice to have you in my corner.* She counted the people in the room. She went and stood beside him. She might not even out the numbers, but she'd give him whatever support she could.

Lorraine finally broke the silence. 'Hello, Cameron.'

'Mum.'

'I wanted to wish you a happy birthday, son, and...' She trailed off as if she wasn't sure what else to say.

Tell him you love him!

'If you really wished me a happy birthday,' Cam

drawled in a voice so hard it made Tess wince, 'you'd have left your other son at home.'

'He wanted to wish you many happy returns too.'

'They say love is blind. Where Lance is concerned, you're living proof.'

'Oh, Cam, please,' Lorraine implored.

'Please what?' He rounded on her. He glared at Lance. 'I want you off my property now!'

Lance flinched, but he held his ground. 'I came to say I'm sorry.'

The silence grew so loud Tess wanted to clap her hands over her ears.

'For?'

She glanced up at Cam uneasily. She didn't like that edge to his voice.

'For...for breaking up your engagement with Fiona. The thing is, I...I love her.' He swallowed. 'But I'm sorry we hurt you.'

'Love her?'

Cam's scorn almost burned the flesh from Tess's arms and it wasn't even directed at her.

'The only person you love, the only person you've ever loved, is yourself.'

Lance flinched.

'The only reason any of you are standing here now is because your farm is in trouble and you want me to bail you out.'

'You're right. Ever since you walked away from the management of the farm it's all gone to hell in a hand basket, but that's not why we're here. We're here because…' He halted, but Fiona nudged him. 'Because I've never been the kind of brother you deserved. I'm sorry for that. But I never really thought you'd turn your back on me and Mum.'

'I haven't turned my back on Mum.'

The unspoken words, *but I've turned my back on you*, hung in the air.

Cam shifted his gaze to Lorraine. 'That said,' he drawled, 'she doesn't seem particularly eager to spend any time in my company.'

Although he hid it well, Tess could feel the hurt emanating from him. She moved a fraction closer.

'Oh, Cameron, honey, it's not that I don't want to spend time with you! But you refuse to step foot over my threshold.'

'The threshold where Lance and Fiona reside,' he pointed out.

'It's this house!' she suddenly blurted out. 'I find it so difficult being here.'

They all stared at her in varying states of astonishment.

'You hate this house?' Cam shifted, frowned. 'But, why?'

Her hand fluttered about her throat. 'That's all in the past now.'

'Obviously it's not or you wouldn't find it so hard being here. Why?' he demanded again.

Lorraine folded her arms as if to shield herself,

and Tess had to fight an urge to go to the older woman.

'You won't like it, Cameron. It does no good to rake over old hurts.'

'The truth,' he demanded in that hard voice Tess found difficult to associate with him.

Lorraine glanced away. Her gaze drifted about the room and she barely suppressed a shudder. 'I was so unhappy here. I…I married your father with such high hopes…'

She dashed away a tear. Tess's throat thickened. Surely Cameron could see what distress he was causing his mother.

'So you had an affair.'

Lorraine drew herself up at that. 'I most certainly did not! I'd left your father for a good eight months before I fell in love with Bill. I left your father because he was unfaithful to me, Cameron. Not once, but multiple times.'

Cam's jaw slackened. 'But he left that house and land for you to use. Even after you'd married another man.'

'Oh, darling, that wasn't due to unrequited love. It was due to remorse. And guilt.'

Tess wanted to take Cam's arm and lead him to a chair to digest the information, to give him time to think and take it all in.

'That's why I never visit this house. It holds so many bad memories for me—a time in my life where

I questioned my very abilities as both a wife and a mother. When I left here I...I thought I would never laugh again. That's why I've refused your dinner invitations, Cameron. I simply can't imagine being in this house and not being overwhelmed again by those old feelings. And since the unfortunate business with Lance and Fiona...well...it's been almost impossible to ask you to dinner at my house. I knew you wouldn't come.'

'Unfortunate?' Cam choked out.

'They didn't do it on purpose, son.'

Cam glared at Lance. 'I don't believe that for a moment,' he said with soft menace. 'I wonder how long Fiona will stick by you, *brother*, when you ruin the farm and have nothing left to your name?'

Lance paled. 'Things have always come easy to you, Cam. You always had good grades, were great at sport and took to farming like it was bred into your bones, but you have no sympathy for those who don't have the same natural aptitude.'

'I have no sympathy with those who sit back and let everybody else do the hard work.'

'It was hell growing up in your shadow!' Lance suddenly yelled. 'I wanted to be just like you, you know that? It's why I took your things. I was hoping they'd give me the key, the magic, but I failed again and again until I decided to stop even trying. And you want to know what the worst thing was? You let me keep all the things I took, when you could've taken them back so easily. Even Fiona. I know you could probably win her back with a snap of your fingers if you put your mind to it, but this time—*this time*—I will fight back.'

'Hey!' Fiona pushed forward to give Lance's arm a shake. 'No, he couldn't. Why do you have so little faith in me?'

'Because you left me for him, so who will you leave him for?'

The words could've been uttered cruelly, contemptuously, but Cam said them with a weariness that simply highlighted their logic.

She stared at Cam with those perfect blue eyes, and Tess wished she could just disappear into the woodwork. She refused to glance up at Cam. She didn't have the heart to deal with the hunger she fully expected to see in his eyes.

'I really wanted to make things work with you,' Fiona said. 'You had such seductive dreams about turning this house into a wonderful family home, but…'

'But you obviously changed your mind and decided my brother was a better bet.'

She shook her head and her perfect blonde ponytail swished about her perfect face in perfect rhythm. 'I came to realise those dreams of yours meant more to you than I ever did. I was just some idea you had of the ideal wife and mother. I needed more than that. I needed you to need me, but you're so self-sufficient, Cam, that I started to think you'd never need anyone.' She glanced at Tess. 'Maybe I was wrong about that.'

Beside her, Cam stiffened. She wanted to drape herself across him and tell Fiona to *back off*! That Cameron was too good for the likes of her. She didn't. That would be a crazy, stupid move, and she was darn sure Cam wouldn't thank her for it if she did. But one thing became increasingly clear. She was fed up with just standing here while these three made excuses for themselves.

'I'll tell you all something for nothing,' she stated so loudly it made everyone jump. 'Cameron has made my family's transition to Bellaroo Creek so much easier than it would otherwise have been. He's one of the best men I have ever met and he's a valued friend.'

True, true and true.

'Furthermore, I think he deserves a whole lot better from all of you.'

'Tess,' he growled.

'No, she's right,' Lorraine said. 'I shouldn't have let stupid memories keep me from coming out here to check on you, Cameron, and to make sure you were doing okay.'

'I didn't need checking up on or looking after.'

She smiled sadly. 'And there you go pushing us away again.'

He rolled his shoulders and frowned. 'I'm not pushing you away.'

'Tess is right, though,' Lance said.

'It's why we wanted to come out here and apologise,' Fiona added. 'And to hold out an olive branch.'

Cameron said nothing, but Tess stood so closely to him she could feel the tension coiling him up tight.

'We're kin, Cam.' Lance held out his hand. 'That has to mean something.'

Tess held her breath, hoping, praying that Cam would accept his brother's proffered hand. She closed her eyes when he gave a harsh laugh.

'Your farm must be in a real state. You're welcome here any time, Mum, but, Lance…you can go to blazes. If I shake your hand now, how long before you turn around and stick the knife in again? How long before you try to steal another canola contract out from under my nose? I'm just waiting to find you rustling my cattle next. But stand warned. If I do I'll be contacting the authorities. You've burned your bridges as far as I'm concerned. Now get out!'

'What about me?' Fiona whispered.

Cam planted his hands on his hips. 'What about you?'

The scent of cut grass wafted about Tess. She drew it slowly into her lungs to counter the nausea churning her stomach. Did Fiona want him back?

'Do you accept my apology? Am I welcome in your home?'

Cam sent Lance a cruel, hard smile. 'You're welcome in my home any time, Fiona.'

Lance turned white. He seized Fiona's hand and stormed from the room.

Lorraine pressed a gift into Cam's hand and then reached up to kiss his cheek. 'It was lovely to see you, Cameron. I just hope we haven't spoiled your day.'

And then she left and Tess could feel all the energy just drain out of her body, leaving her limp and wrecked. It must be a hundred times worse for Cam. She moved to a chair, pressed her hands together between her knees. Her pink party dress suddenly seemed totally out of place. She eyed Cam carefully. He hadn't moved. She cleared her throat. 'Are you okay?'

He rounded on her then. 'That was all your doing, wasn't it?'

Her jaw dropped.

He flung an arm out, pacing from one side of the room to the other. 'I should've known little Miss Fix-it wouldn't be able to mind her own business, that she'd need to interfere.'

She shot to her feet. The roller coaster of emotions she'd experienced this afternoon crashing through her now. 'Well, even if I did—' which she hadn't, but she'd rather walk on broken glass now than admit it '—I sure didn't make things worse. Oh, no, you accomplished that all on your own!'

He swung back to her. 'Are you telling me you actually believed that line he fed me?'

She planted herself directly in front of him. 'Yes, I do.' And strangely enough she did. It was only now when he was deprived of his brother that Lance could see all that Cam meant to him, and how much he needed him. 'But even if I didn't,' she suddenly found herself shouting, 'he's your brother and he deserves the benefit of the doubt!'

'Just because you feel guilty about letting Sarah down doesn't give you the right to go meddling in my life! Fixing my situation won't be a form of restitution, you know.'

She sucked in a breath. 'At least I'm not hiding from life.'

'What do you call turning away from your music?'

She clenched her hands. 'At least I'm not afraid to let love in my life. At least I put people first!'

Neither of their voices had lost any of their volume and the walls practically rang with their shouts.

'That's just as well because you know nothing about chickens!'

'At least I know how to throw a decent party! Me!' She thumped her chest. '*Me* has got the hang of country hospitality in under a month. You haven't got the hang of it your whole life!'

'Your grammar sucks!'

'And your manners suck!'

She glared. He glared.

She bit her lip. His lips started to twitch.

She snorted. *'Me has got?'*

He rolled his eyes. 'I can't believe I made that chicken crack.'

And suddenly they were both roaring with laughter.

And then Cameron pulled her right into his arms and kissed her.

CHAPTER NINE

RAW, BURNING NEED blazed a path of fire through the very centre of Cam's being and shot out in every direction. He'd ached to kiss this woman ever since... ever since he'd clapped eyes on her. But he'd burned harder and fiercer with that need since the first kiss they'd shared. And he was tired of fighting it.

He revelled in the sweet softness of Tess's lips and the way they opened up at his demand—so sweet and giving as if she sensed his hunger and wanted to assuage it. So unselfish.

The realisation made him slow the kiss down, gentle it until she could catch up with him. Loosening his hold on her nape, he slid his hand through the dark cap of her hair and caressed the skin behind her ear in a slow circular motion, and then followed with his mouth. A shudder rippled through her, filling him with satisfaction, increasing his hunger, but he refused to speed up to meet that demand.

He wanted Tess with him. All the way. He wanted her smiling and satisfied...sated and delighted. A resolution he nearly lost the battle with when her grip tightened on his arms and she moved in closer to press all her softness against him.

He tugged gently on her ear lobe. She gasped and arched into him. He grinned a lazy grin and did it again. She smelled of jellybeans and cake. Breathing her in was a treat in itself. The grin disappeared when she shifted restlessly against him, one of her hands plunging into his hair, her other arm winding around his neck.

He lost all sense of himself then, all sense of time. His mouth found hers and he fell into her, losing himself in the experience of kissing her, touching her, filling himself up with her essence like a man gorging on some vital nutrient he'd been lacking but had suddenly found.

The hunger built and built until kissing and touching was no longer enough. He needed—

A groan broke from him when she tore her lips from his and wrenched herself out of his arms. She stumbled to a sofa on the other side of the room. Seizing a cushion, she hugged it to her chest.

His chest rose and fell as if he'd spent the last hour roping yearlings. He wanted to stride over to where Tess sat, haul her back into his arms and propel this encounter through to its natural conclusion. He almost did, but common sense reasserted itself. Ty and Krissie were somewhere on the premises. This was not the ideal time for making love to Tess.

He bit back an oath. 'I'm sorry. The timing on that could've been better.'

She didn't say anything. He wanted her to look at him, but she didn't do that either.

He dragged in a breath, adjusted his stance and tried to quieten the stampeding of his blood. 'Would you like to have dinner with me tonight? Jenny would love to babysit the kids and—'

'No.'

He blinked.

She plumped the cushion up and set it back to the sofa. 'There won't ever be a good time for us, Cameron.'

'But—'

'Do you think I'm the kind of woman who jumps willy-nilly into bed with men I know I have no future with?'

'No, I—'

She walked across and poked him in the chest. 'Do you want me to fall in love with you so you can then break my heart? Will that mend your wounded ego and make you feel powerful and manly again? Will that show Lance that you're over what he did to you?'

Her eyes blazed with a fire he hadn't witnessed before, but her words left him chilled. 'No!' How could she put such a dreadful interpretation on his desire for her? 'You're beautiful, Tess. I find you fascinating and irresistible. I love kissing you.'

Colour flared in her cheeks. She backed up a step. 'That may well be, but it's been an emotional day. I refuse to be the distraction you need to distance yourself from all that's happened this afternoon.'

He stabbed a finger at her. 'You're more than a distraction!' She was wonderful and warm and she could make him laugh even when he was livid.

She folded her arms and lifted her chin. 'How much more?'

A chill trickled down his backbone. For a short time today this woman had brought his old dream roaring back to life. She'd made him wonder if it were still possible. The arrival of his mother, Lance and Fiona had dashed that, had forced him to face reality again.

'You still have no intention of forgiving Lance. You're determined to hold on to your bitterness. What would it hurt to just let it go?'

His gut clenched. 'How can you even ask that?'

She pressed a hand to her forehead. 'There's absolutely no point to this conversation. You have no intention of staying in Bellaroo Creek anyway, have you?'

He straightened and shoved his shoulders back. He wasn't being made a fool of a second time. Not by Lance. Not by Tess. Not by anyone.

She gave a short laugh, obviously reading the resolution in his face. 'Well, in the meantime I won't let you turn me into some toy you can play with. I might've let my sister down, but I don't deserve that. And the children certainly deserve better.'

He wanted Tess in every way a man would want a woman. If she were free and unencumbered he'd ask her to come to Africa with him. For fun. For adventure. No strings. His chest clenched. Maybe...

He closed his eyes. What was he thinking? Tess was all strings and he wanted no part of that. Besides she wanted the impossible. Forgive Lance? No chance. He made himself take a physical step away from her. His chest hurt, his groin ached, but he held firm.

Without even glancing at him, she headed for the door.

'Tess...' He could hardly speak for the bitterness that coated his tongue and lined his throat.

She turned in the doorway.

'Whatever else has happened, you've not let Sarah down. You love her kids as if they're your own. You're giving them not just a good life but a great life. You've brought them laughter and joy and hope for the future. You never let Sarah down. If you'd known the true state of affairs you'd have returned home as soon as you could. And I don't doubt for a single moment that she knew that. Saying you let her down by not returning home sooner is the same as saying she let you down because she didn't tell you the truth sooner. Nobody let anybody down.'

She gripped her hands together, her eyes wide and wounded. He wished—

He cut the thought off. 'There's only one issue that I suspect would bring Sarah pain. How do you think she'd feel if she knew you'd turned your back on your music because of her?'

The confusion that flared in her eyes made him ache to go to her, to comfort her. But she didn't want the kind of comfort he offered and he could hardly blame her. When she turned and left, he let her go.

Cam avoided Tess's house for the next week. She attended his judo class on Wednesday. When they'd heard she was doing the class, another two mums had signed up too. The three of them had spent the majority of the class in fits of giggles. He hadn't spoken to her one-on-one, though.

Instinct told him she needed time. He sure did. Time to rebuild his defences. Time to reinforce his plans for the future. Time to forget the impact of their kisses. Because after vowing not to, he'd almost fallen under the spell of that old dream again. Tess brought out that old weakness in him, and he was determined to fight it with everything he had.

Out of sight, though, didn't mean out of mind.

And there was still the issue of her vegetable garden. His debt to her wouldn't be cleared until he'd finished that.

The following Saturday he loaded the tray of his

ute with all the tools he'd need—shovels, picks, hoes and a generous amount of cow manure—and headed for Tess's. One good day should see the vegetable bed finished. He'd help her with the planting and give her tips on how to look after it.

And then he could walk away. Job done. Debt cleared.

He pulled in a breath when he arrived, and then set off towards the back of her house. *Don't think about that kiss!* Work, that was what he had to think about. Work and digging and—

He rounded the side of the house and then pulled up short, unable to move another step.

Tess and the kids were dancing around the backyard, singing along to a pop song on the radio. And it wasn't just any old singing and dancing. His chest clenched. They jumped and twirled and swooped with abandon. With complete unadulterated joy at being alive. As if this moment was the best moment that had ever existed and they were going to clutch it and hold it close and cherish it and live it before it could slip away.

It filled him with a yearning that almost buckled him at the knees.

Tess's hips swayed and shook in a sexy rhythm and his mouth dried and his blood pounded. Her simple delight in the dance and the way she occasionally caught one of the children's eyes and how their pleasure fed each other's left him breathless. He'd never seen anything like it.

He'd never experienced anything like it.

His heart started to thump and an ache pounded behind his eyes. He would *never* experience anything like it. This kind of exuberance, rapture, was alien to his family.

Duty, responsibility and self-reliance—those were all the things he'd been taught to value. Not joy. And no matter how much he might hunger for the same kind of closeness with his family that Tess and the kids shared, he knew it was beyond his reach.

Fiona had taught him that. Trying to reach for these heights with her had revealed it for the sham it had been. He had to stick to what he did know—duty, responsibility and self-reliance.

Without a word, he backed up a step, turned and headed for his car.

Tess spun around, arms outstretched as the song came to an end, feeling alive and young and grateful for Ty and Krissie's laughter, when a flash of blue disappearing around the side of the house caught her eye.

She acted on instinct. 'Hey, Cam!' She tripped around the side of the house.

He froze. He didn't turn around. Her heart surged against her rib cage. His back beckoned—so strong and muscled. So capable. Her fingers curled against her palms. 'Anything we can do for you?'

'Hey, Cam!' Ty came rushing around the side of the house with Barney in close pursuit. 'Look, I taught Barney how to shake hands.'

Cameron turned to watch the trick. He smiled, but it didn't reach his eyes. 'That's brilliant, Ty. He's one smart dog.'

Those shadows in his eyes chafed at her. They made her want to go to him and offer herself to him, to offer the kind of comfort he wanted from her.

She glanced at Ty and Krissie, planted her feet and remained where she was.

'I, uh…' He rose from patting an ecstatic Barney. 'Thought I might get a start on digging the bed for your vegetable garden.'

Bed? It brought a whole different picture to her mind that had nothing to do with gardening or vegetables. Heat that had nothing to do with the exertion of dancing surged into her cheeks. It took a moment to unknot her tongue. 'That'd be great,' she finally managed. 'If you can spare the time, that is?'

'Right.'

He didn't move. She didn't move. The air between them vibrated with all that remained unspoken.

With a superhuman effort she managed to shake herself out from beneath the heavy, suffocating blanket that tried to descend over her. She clapped her hands. 'Right! Let's help Cam unload his tools.'

They all set to work. Digging, she decided an hour later, wasn't a bad antidote to restlessness. Other than to issue instructions or to check his directions, she and Cam barely spoke. But as they worked side by side together the tension slowly dissipated. She liked having him in her backyard again. She frowned at that thought. He'd been a great friend.

He'd be a better lover.

Whoa!

She pushed the thought away, thrust her shovel into the ground, and pushed her hands into the small of her back, groaning as her muscles protested.

Cam sent her a grin that filled her to the brim with renewed energy. 'Sore?'

'No wonder you're so fit if you do this kind of work day in and day out. All I can say is thank God it's lunchtime. I'll go rustle up something to eat.'

A short while later they all sat in the sun munching sandwiches and apples.

Krissie glanced up. 'Auntie Tess?'

'What, chickadee?'

'It's a big vegetable garden, isn't it?'

'Well, I'm not an expert on vegetable gardens, but I think ours is pretty much the perfect size.'

'So can we grow marigolds in there too? Will there be room? Did you know they were Mummy's favourite?'

Yes, she did know. Her throat tightened. She swallowed. 'I think there'll be oodles of room for marigolds. I think marigolds will be the perfect addition to our vegetable garden.'

Krissie, Ty, and the animals all ran off to play.

Cam shook his head. 'You can't eat marigolds.'

She couldn't tell if he was vexed with her or not. 'They do look pretty in a vase, though.' And for taking out to a grave. She eased back on the blanket to survey him more fully. 'Do you always choose the common-sense option?'

'I work the land. Planting forty hectares of marigolds instead of canola will not earn me my crust.'

'What a sight it'd be though.'

He suddenly smiled. 'Wait until the canola blossoms.' He gestured out in front of them at the newly ploughed fields that stretched over a low hill in the distance. 'It will be bright yellow for as far as you can see.'

'Magic,' she breathed. Then she frowned. 'But you won't be here to see it?'

He shook his head.

Wouldn't he miss that? Didn't he want to see the fruits of his labour? She bit the questions back. They'd carefully avoided any mention of the personal today, had found a comfortable footing with each other, and she didn't want to ruin it. 'I'll take a photo and have Fraser send it to you,' she said instead.

She was just about to tip the dregs of her mug of tea out when Ty and Krissie came up. She could tell from the fact they walked rather than ran and by the serious expressions on their faces that they'd just 'conferred' about something. 'What's up, chickadees?' She kept her voice deliberately light and cheerful.

'When are we going to have Mummy's…' Ty frowned, obviously searching for the right word.

'Memorial?' she asked softly.

They both nodded and knelt down on the blanket in front of her.

'Well, Mrs Pritchard is organising a plot for us, and I expect to hear from her about that in the next couple of weeks. Then I'll speak to Reverend Wilkinson, who'll perform the service, but he's only out this way every second week.' How long was a piece of string? Things moved at a different pace in the country. 'So I'm expecting it'll be maybe in a month, possibly two.'

'So, sorta soon?' Ty checked.

She nodded.

They leapt up, evidently satisfied. 'But while we're on the subject…' she started, her throat drying.

They stared at her for a moment and then sank back down to the blanket. Her chest clenched. Maybe she should let this subject rest. Instinct, though, told her ignoring it wouldn't be right.

'Okay, chickadees, we need to talk about your daddy.' Ty's eyes grew wide and wary. Her stomach started to churn. 'Do we want to bury his ashes too? Do we want to put them in the same plot as Mummy's?'

'No!' Ty shot to his feet. 'I hate him! He killed Mummy!'

The blood drained from her face. Her hands started to shake. 'Ty, honey, that's not true.' His bottom lip wobbled. He stood there pale and shaking. Her heart lurched and her eyes stung. She wanted to reach out and hug him to her, but she sensed any such movement would send him running. 'That's not true, Ty. I promise you. You know Daddy was sick.' She'd tried to explain it, but, truly, how much were they expected to understand? Especially when Tess could barely accept it herself. 'It was an accident.'

'No, it wasn't! I heard him say he was going to kill her. He drove into that tree on purpose!'

Tears poured down his face. They started to pour down hers too. 'He only said those things because he was sick. He didn't mean them. And I know he didn't drive the car deliberately into the tree, Ty, because he wasn't the one driving—Mummy was.'

His fists clenched. His face turned red. 'No!'

She tried to take him into her arms, but he wheeled out of her reach and raced away. She started to her feet, but Cam's hand on her shoulder stopped her.

'I'll go after him,' he said quietly with a nod towards Krissie.

She turned and found her little niece with her face buried in the blanket and her shoulders shaking. With a lump in her throat the size of a teapot, Tess lifted the child into her lap and wrapped her arms tight around her.

Ty didn't go far. He'd raced around the front of the house to fling himself down full length on the veranda.

Cam sat next to the distraught boy and hauled him into his arms so he could cry against his chest.

His throat thickened as he rubbed a hand up and down Ty's back, trying to impart whatever comfort he could. So much grief and pain. These kids had been through so much. Tess was doing a great job, but...

He thought back to this morning's image of them all dancing. Tess was doing a *brilliant* job. It was those moments of joy that would help Ty and Krissie through the hardship of their grief and create bonds that would link them together as a family. He ached to take away all their pain—Tess's included—but that wasn't possible. All he could do was offer his friendship and hope it helped.

Tess. His mind rang with her. She was trying to do so much on her own. And she was achieving so much. If only she could see that she didn't have to lose herself in the process.

Eventually Ty's sobs eased to hiccups. A couple of minutes after that he pushed away from Cam's chest to stare up in his face.

'How you doing, buddy?' Cam asked, his chest cramping at the small, tear-stained face. He found himself wanting to protect this young boy from every kind of harm. All of Tess's fussing suddenly made perfect sense.

'Do you think Auntie Tess is right?' he said without preamble.

He'd give away Kurrajong Station in an instant if it'd mean sparing them all of this. He met Ty's gaze. 'Has your aunt Tess ever lied to you about anything else?'

Ty considered that for a long moment. 'No,' he finally said.

'Then do you really think she'd lie to you about this?'

He considered that too. 'She doesn't want me and Krissie to be mad with our dad.' He glared. 'But I am. I'm really mad.'

'Yeah, I get that.'

Ty gazed up at him, eyes wary. 'You do?'

'Sure I do. Your dad hurt you and Krissie and your mum. It'd make me angry too.'

'Auntie Tess said he was sick.'

'I think your auntie Tess is right. And you know what else I think? I think that your dad would be very glad that he can't hurt you any more.'

'Even though he's dead?'

Cam nodded. 'Even then.'

'You think he loved us?'

'I think he loved you all very much, Ty. I think he just wasn't able to show it any more.'

Ty rested his head against Cam's shoulder. The trust awed him. The warm weight cracked open a gulf of yearning inside him. He closed his eyes. He understood Ty's anger. It was the same as his anger at Lance. Except Ty's dad had been sick. Lance had no such excuse.

Eventually Ty pushed away and climbed out of Cam's lap. He missed the warmth and the weight immediately.

'I'm going to go and give Auntie Tess a hug.'

'I think that's an excellent plan.'

He followed Ty around to the backyard to find Tess and Krissie, now with Fluffy on her lap, talking quietly on the blanket. Tess turned at their approach. Without a word she opened her arms and Ty raced into them.

What if, like Ty and Krissie's father, Lance died in a car accident? The ground shifted beneath his feet. He planted his legs more firmly and bit back a curse. Lance had burned his proverbial bridges. He was nothing to Cam any more.

That assertion, though, didn't ease the burn in Cam's heart.

He forced himself to focus on the tableau in front of him. Tess held Ty for several long moments and then rose, holding him in her arms. She hitched her head in the direction of the house and Cam nodded, settling down on the blanket beside Krissie.

She glanced up at him with those big brown eyes that were identical to Tess's. With a cluck and a flutter, Fluffy freed herself to scratch about in the grass.

Krissie moved closer and curled up against him as if it were the most natural thing in the world. 'You okay, pet?'

She nodded. 'My daddy was very sick, you know?'

'So I understand, honey.'

'It's very sad,' she whispered, leaning into him. 'And I think we should bury him with Mummy and maybe he'll be happy again.'

She was five, but her generosity and ability to forgive stole his breath. 'I think that's a real nice idea, sweetheart.'

He wasn't sure for how long they sat there, but when Tess materialised in front of him, he glanced down to find Krissie fast asleep. Tess went to take her from him, but he shook his head. 'Let me. You lead the way.'

They put Krissie to bed. He followed Tess back into the kitchen. She grabbed two beers from the fridge and handed him one before leading the way back outside again.

'You okay?' he asked. She looked pale and lines of weariness fanned out from her eyes. She looked as if she could do with a nap herself.

She settled on the blanket, stretching her legs out

in front of her before glancing up at him. 'Some days I feel as if we're merely lurching from one catastrophe to another.'

He lowered himself down beside her. It suddenly shamed him to think how he'd tried to seduce her last weekend. She had so much to deal with. 'I held Ty while he cried his heart out and all I wanted to do was make things better for him. I know that's impossible. I don't know how you're managing to do all this with such grace.'

She opened her beer. 'I'm not sure there's much grace involved.'

'I think you're doing an incredible job.'

She turned those eyes on him. Eyes the same as Krissie's. He had absolutely no intention of trying to seduce her again, but what if she moved in close and curled up against him the way Krissie had? He couldn't get the thought out of his mind.

He forced his gaze away. 'I will tell you something,' he managed. 'Nobody could get them through this as well as you are.'

She took a long pull on her beer. 'Some days are better than others. The gaps between the bad days are getting longer.'

He read her unspoken hope that eventually there wouldn't be any more bad days, but both of them knew bad days came and went. Ty and Krissie, as they got older, would simply learn to deal with those bad days more effectively. With Tess's help.

'So...' She studied him. 'Are you okay?' She asked as if she could sense the confusion bubbling just beneath the surface. It reminded him how well attuned they were to each other's moods. It reminded him that he *wasn't* going to attempt to seduce her again.

'Yeah, sure.'

But even as he said the words he knew they were a lie.

He frowned. 'Krissie...'

She watched him closely, as closely as he often caught her watching the children. It made the ache around his heart ease for some unaccountable reason. 'What about Krissie?'

'Something she said...' He scratched a hand back through his hair. 'She said she thought that if her father was buried with her mother, then maybe he'd be happy again.' His frown grew. 'She *wants* him to be happy.'

'Of course she does. He was her father. She loved him.'

'But he hurt her and Ty so badly.'

'Your father was unfaithful to your mother, but does that make you love him any less?'

His mother's revelation had shocked him, had made him rethink all he'd thought he knew about his father—but, no, it didn't affect the love he bore for him.

'I think a part of Krissie remembers the good

times before her father's accident, when they were all happy and life was how it should've been. I think Sarah helped keep those memories alive.'

'You've forgiven him too, haven't you?'

She stared down at her beer and nodded.

He leapt up and started to pace. 'How can you? How can you find that in yourself after everything he did to your sister?' He knew she'd loved Sarah. 'And to those kids? I know how much you love them.'

'I don't see why loving them means I should hate Bruce. I can't forget that Sarah hadn't given up on him. I know *she* still loved him. I can't forget all the years he made her happy or their joy when the children were born. They—'

She broke off to stare at her drink. 'He didn't go looking for that accident. He didn't deserve what happened to him. He'd been a loving husband and father up till that point. And I'm proud of Sarah for sticking by him.'

He opened his mouth but she held up a hand. 'Yes, she should've gotten the children away from that situation sooner, but I'm proud of her for having the courage to try to find help for the man she loved. My sister loved him, Cameron. I cannot hate him. I...I just can't.'

He's your brother and he deserves the benefit of the doubt!

He collapsed back down beside her, her words of

last weekend echoing through him. He knew precisely where Krissie's generosity and her big heart came from—from her auntie Tess. 'No wonder you think me a hard, unfeeling brute.'

'I think no such thing!'

'Lance.'

Just one word but comprehension dawned in those melt-a-man eyes of hers. 'That's a bit different. You're an adult and so is Lance, even if he has been acting like a petulant teenager.' She smoothed the rug and glanced away. 'He's learning a very hard lesson now, though.'

I think a part of Krissie remembers the good times.

Cam scowled at the ground. There had been good times, but...

'I think it'll probably be good for him in the long run. He relies too heavily on his charm, and I suspect your mother has shielded him far more than has been good for him. A bit of hard work and a whole lot of worry may make a man out of him yet.'

His head came up. 'Steady on, Tess, he's not that bad.'

There were days when Lance had made life hell. There'd also been days when he'd made Cam laugh until his sides had hurt. It was why Cam had put up with the hell days—because nobody else in the family had ever laughed all that much. That laughter had been worth a lot.

She leaned back, stared down her nose at him. 'Do I hear you defending him?'

Was he?

If anything happened to Lance while he was in Africa… Cam swallowed. What if something happened to him while he was away? Was this really how he meant to leave things?

He frowned and finally cracked open his beer. 'I guess I am.'

She arched an eyebrow. 'Is that significant?'

He dragged in a breath. 'If Krissie can forgive her dad…' He shook his head. 'Lord, Tess, I can't be shown up by a five-year-old, now, can I?'

'It'd be very poor form,' she agreed.

Somewhere inside him a smile started to build. He held his beer towards her. She clinked it in a silent toast.

CHAPTER TEN

Tess wanted to leap to her feet and dance. She wanted to hug Cam.

She suspected the dancing would prove the lesser of two evils.

A new calm had settled over him, certain shadows had retreated from his eyes—not all, but some—and his shoulders had lost their angry edge.

She surveyed them and bit her lip. In fact, they looked broad and scrumptious.

Cam cleared his throat and she realised with a start that she'd been staring at them for too long. She snapped her gaze away and lifted her beer to her lips. 'If you want my two cents' worth…' she started before taking a sip.

'Which you'll give me, even if I don't.'

The grin he shot her and the effortlessness with which he teased her filled her with such a fluttery nonsense of wings she was in danger of floating two feet above the ground. She clutched a handful of blanket and held tight.

'What's your two cents, Tess?'

She surveyed him over the rim of her beer. 'I think you should pay your family a visit tomorrow afternoon.'

'Why?'

'The sooner the better, don't you think?'

He stared at her for a long moment. 'And?'

'And I'll be there,' she finally 'fessed up. She wanted to be there when he faced his family too. She wanted to make sure Lorraine, Lance and Fiona didn't take advantage of him. 'Last weekend at your party it was as if it were you against them and the rest of the world. That's not true. You have friends and I think both you and they should acknowledge that fact.'

Also, her being there would create a subtle confusion she was eager to encourage. Cameron might love Fiona to her dying day, but neither Lance nor Fiona had to know that. They had no right to crow in triumph. It wouldn't hurt anyone to think Cameron had well and truly moved on.

It could hurt you.

She shrugged the thought off. She knew the truth—Cam was leaving. Forewarned was forearmed. She could protect her heart.

'I'm dropping Ty and Krissie off at a birthday party and then popping by Lorraine's to discuss the memorial service. Apparently Lance and Fiona plan to be there to offer their...' She shrugged and rolled her eyes.

'Moral support?'

She bared her teeth. 'Something like that.'

He started to laugh. 'So who exactly is helping who in this scenario?'

She couldn't help but grin back at him. 'Why don't we call it a joint effort?'

His grin was slow and easy and it could make a woman's heart kick straight into triple time without any warning at all. 'What time are you supposed to be out there?'

'One-thirty.'

'I have a few things to do in the morning, but... I'll be out there by two.'

'Excellent.'

'C'mon.' He nodded towards the garden bed. 'Time to get back to work.' He helped her to her feet and she tried to ignore the strength of his hands, tried to ignore the heat he exuded, and the fresh smell of cut grass.

She averted her gaze from the strong, lean promise of his back and threw herself into attacking the ground with the assorted instruments of destruction currently within reach.

'Well, Tess,' Lorraine said, leaning back in the padded wicker sofa that graced her generous back patio, 'that should all be remarkably easy to arrange.'

Tess had just outlined the simple service she and the children had agreed upon.

'No Herculean feats to be performed,' Lance said with a smile.

He almost looked disappointed, as if he sensed Tess's reservations about his character and wanted to prove himself in her eyes. Who knew? Maybe he did. But if she needed any Herculean tasks performed she'd ask his brother, thank you very much.

Fiona leant forward to top up Tess's teacup. 'Do have a scone,' she urged, as if unstinting hospitality might melt Tess's reserve.

It'd take more than a scone and a cup of tea. What this pair had done to Cam—

It's none of your business. She had no right holding a grudge against this pair. Especially when she'd been urging Cam not to and—

Her teacup wobbled. None of her business? Everything to do with Cam felt like her business.

Because he's helped you so much, helped you, Ty and Krissie feel a part of Bellaroo Creek.

That was right. That was all it was.

Her heart started to thump. Why, then, when he smiled at her did her heart grow wings? Why when his eyes practically devoured her did she feel like the most desirable woman on earth? Why when she kissed him was it better than making music?

She'd told herself she'd wanted to be here today to support him, but it wasn't the whole truth, was it?

She set her tea down before she could spill it. She'd wanted to be here today to prevent Fiona from getting her perfect pretty little claws into him again. She'd wanted to stake her claim.

Because she'd fallen in love with him.

Her heart throbbed. Her temples pounded. Cam had made it clear to her that she had no claim to stake. Hadn't she been listening?

Of course she'd been listening! She seized a pumpkin scone and bit into it viciously. But how could a woman not fall in love with a man like Cam? He had the biggest heart of any person she'd ever met. He did so much for others, and all of it without fanfare. He had the kind of grin that could melt a woman's resolutions in a heartbeat and the kind of physique that could have her fantasising in Technicolor.

He was so…much. He was everything. And she loved him.

The acknowledgement calmed the dervishes careening through her blood. A hard black ache settled in her heart instead. She set her pumpkin scone back to her plate.

Cam rounded the corner of the veranda and found his family and Tess seated in front of him. In the warm sunshine and the filtered light from a wisteria vine, the tableau looked inviting and almost summery—even with the cool of autumn in the air.

Tess, though, looked pale and his heart lurched for her. Organising this memorial service must be hell. She glanced up and her face relaxed into a smile of pure pleasure. It immediately buoyed him up. He couldn't remember any woman's smile affecting him the way Tess's did. Not even Fiona's.

'Hello, Cameron.'

'Tess.'

His mother shot to her feet, delight lighting her face. 'Cam!'

He moved down the length of the veranda and kissed her cheek. 'Hello, Mum.'

Lance stood more slowly. He nodded to Cam and then turned to Lorraine. 'There's some work I should get done in the eastern paddock.'

Fiona jumped up too. 'I'll help.'

There was no denying that they were trying to make room for him, trying to make things less awkward. He appreciated the effort. Tess had been right. They deserved the benefit of the doubt. 'I'd like the two of you to stay, if you don't mind.'

A tremulous smile appeared on Fiona's lips. It left him unmoved and he suddenly frowned. When precisely had he fallen out of love with her? His heart started to pound. Or had she been right? Had he been more in love with his dream of filling Kurrajong Station with laughter and with a family?

Lance sat when Fiona tugged him back down to the seat beside her. His blue eyes filled with a hope he desperately tried to hide, but Cam had always been able to read his little brother.

Until he'd turned his back on him.

He glanced at Tess and she held a hand out to him. He took it without thinking, squeezed it before releasing it to take the lone chair at right angles to her. The only other spare seat was beside his mother. It wasn't that he wanted to shun her. He just wanted to face his family square on during this conversation—read their faces, gauge their reactions.

'You wanted to speak to us about something, Cameron?' his mother asked.

'I've been thinking about your visit last weekend, and it has to be said that I was discourteous and churlish in response to your offer of an olive branch. If the offer still stands, I'd like to accept it.'

'It still stands!' Lance shot to his feet and thrust his hand towards Cam.

Cam rose and shook it. With a nod he took his seat again. He met Tess's warm gaze, recognised her unspoken approbation. It made him push his shoulders back and lift his chin. Her innate generosity and the sacrifices she'd made had helped him see sense. More than that, though, she'd made him believe he was worth more than he'd ever credited before.

He turned back to Lance before he could become too preoccupied with the dusky fullness of Tess's bottom lip. 'This is just a start. It's going to take me a while to trust you again.'

'I know.' Lance squared his shoulders. 'But it's a start, and I'm not going to screw up this time.'

Cam stretched a leg out. 'Now to the financial situation of this station. I'm not just going to bail you guys out. I'm not a bank and I have my own place to consider. But—' he glanced at his mother '—I am prepared to buy a fifty per cent share of the property and to invest in improving it.'

She bit her lip and nodded. It was an acknowledgement, not an acceptance. This was business. This wouldn't be her ideal scenario, but interest-free loans and working for this station gratis were a thing of the past.

He glanced back at Lance. 'Are you fair dinkum about giving farming a proper go?'

'Yes.'

'Then I'm prepared to pay you a wage to train under Fraser for the next two years. If Mum does decide to sell me half the property, and if you prove yourself, I will let you buy back my share of this station for whatever the current market value is.'

Lance swallowed and nodded. 'I accept.' Fiona nudged him and he broke into a grin. 'In fact, I'm darn grateful, but…'

He had to stop his lips from twisting. Here it came. 'But?'

'Cam, I'd rather work under you than Fraser.'

The steel momentarily left his spine. It was the last thing he'd expected Lance to say. It brought home to him the depth of the younger man's resolution. A breath eased out of him. 'I'm afraid that won't be possible.'

His mother leaned towards him. 'Why not, darling?'

'Because I won't be here.' His gut tightened and he couldn't look at Tess. 'I've accepted a field assignment to Africa with the Feed the World programme.'

'For how long?'

'Two years.'

To his right, he heard Tess's quick intake of breath and his chest started to ache.

'When do you leave?' Lance burst out.

'The end of next month.'

And then all hell broke loose as his mother, Lance and Fiona all broke out in loud voices, talking over each other as they remonstrated with him. Tess leaned across to touch his arm. 'Will you stay at least until the memorial service?'

He didn't know when the service was scheduled, but he knew she wouldn't try to trick him into staying any longer. He trusted her. 'Yes.'

'Thank you. It'll mean so much to Ty and Krissie.'

And her?

'And me,' she added as if she could read his mind.

Then she stood. 'Honestly,' she snapped to his family, 'stop all this nonsense. All his life Cameron has looked after you lot. All his life he's done things for other people. Stop being so selfish and think of him for once. He's entitled to follow his dream and you as his family should be supporting him rather than bellyaching at him and making things difficult.'

She was fierce and fabulous and he suddenly wanted to laugh with sheer exhilaration. But when she turned to smile at him he wanted to close his eyes. He recognised what glowed in the gorgeous brown depths of her eyes. Love.

Love for him.

And he had absolutely no intention of accepting it, of returning it, and that knowledge was there in her eyes too.

Bile burned his throat. Why hadn't he taken more care around her? She was the one person in Bellaroo Creek who wanted what was truly best for him—without agenda and without reference to her own needs or desires. He'd rather cut off his right arm than hurt her. A giant vise squeezed his heart. He hadn't meant for it to happen, but a fat lot of good that would do her in the months to come.

He opened his mouth. He wanted to offer her some form of comfort. Only he knew that'd be useless. Worse than useless.

He dragged a hand back through his hair. She'd wanted to be here today to shield him in whatever way she could from Lance and Fiona's betrayal. That all seemed so small and petty now. If only there'd been someone looking out for her!

'Tess is right,' his mother finally said, waving everyone back to their seats. 'Again.'

'Again?' he found himself asking.

'The day of the working bee at the cemetery I mentioned to Tess how nice it was to see you there.' Lorraine bit her lip. 'She said I might want to mention that to you, and it made me suddenly see how... unsupportive I must've seemed to you. Frankly, I was mortified.'

And because of Tess he now knew why his mother had stayed away from Kurrajong Station for all these years.

'She gave me a right set down that day too,' Lance said. 'Demanded to know if I'd ever actually apologised for my appalling behaviour.' He grimaced. 'It was the kick in the pants I needed.'

Cam turned to stare at Tess. She screwed up her nose. 'I tried really hard to mind my own business, but...'

He leaned across and covered her hand with his. 'I'm glad you didn't. I want you to know that all this—' he gestured around the table '—is due to you. And I'm grateful.'

'So am I.' Lorraine rose and embraced Tess. 'My darling girl, not only are you helping save my beloved town, you've helped save my family.'

With her arm about Tess's waist, she turned to Cam. 'Darling, of course you must do what your heart tells you. You've been involved with the Feed the World programme for so long, and I know you've made a real difference in the lives of those less fortunate than us. It's selfish of us to want to keep you to ourselves, but you must never forget that you always have a home here with us.'

He leant across and kissed his mother's cheek. 'I won't forget.' But it was Tess's fragrance he drew into his lungs as he moved away.

'I think it's beyond time I made a fresh pot of tea. Could you give me a hand, Fiona, dear?'

Cam turned to Tess. He wanted to say something—something that would tell her how much he appreciated all she had done, and how sorry he was for the rest of it.

Her smile and the tiny shake of her head forestalled him. 'I think it's all worked out exactly the way it should've, don't you?'

No.

Oh, it had for him and his mother, and for Lance and Fiona, but not for her. Not in the way she deserved.

'I'm mighty glad you came around today, Cam.'

Lance's words reminded him that he and Tess weren't alone. And he didn't want to say or do anything that might embarrass her in front of Lance or cue anybody in on her pain. Tess was like him. She'd not want a broken heart on display for all and sundry to exclaim and pick over. He could at least do that much for her.

He turned to his brother. 'So am I.' And he meant it more than he'd thought he would.

'Say.' Lance pointed, leading him to the edge of the veranda. 'See that colt in the home paddock? Do you think he's ready for breaking?'

Cam watched the colt moving over the grass with an easy gait and his tail held high. 'Your call, Lance, but I'd be inclined to give him another six months.'

When Cam turned back, Tess was gone. Every atom in his body shouted at him to go after her. He remained where he was. In his heart he knew there was nothing he could say that would make an atom of difference to either one of them. Letting her go was harder than going after her, but it was also kinder.

Where Tess was concerned he'd already done enough harm.

CHAPTER ELEVEN

TESS WORKED HARD at making the memorial service a celebration of Sarah's and Bruce's lives. The scheduled day dawned cold and still, with barely a breath of breeze to stir the leaves in the Kurrajong trees. Cameron's canola had been planted and, while winter had arrived, the blue skies and constant sunshine made her feel as if she, Ty and Krissie were moving into a smoother, calmer period. Truly a new beginning.

Even though she missed Sarah every single day.

Even though whenever she thought of Cameron leaving Bellaroo Creek her heart trembled and her throat would close over.

Still, at least she would know that somewhere in the world Cam was following his heart. If his heart could never belong to her, then she just wanted him happy.

When the day of the memorial service dawned—with Cam due to leave Bellaroo Creek the very next day—Tess bounced out of bed and lifted her chin.

She had so much—a home, two beautiful children, and a bright future. Today she meant to count her blessings, not her sorrows.

The entire town turned out for the memorial service. The women wore their best dresses, and while not all the men owned suits, they all wore ties. It touched her to the very centre of her being.

The minister gave a brief but heartfelt sermon. Lorraine led them all in a stirring version of 'Amazing Grace'. Tess, with Ty and Krissie at her side, gave a eulogy—she spoke about Sarah's generosity, her love for her family, and how much she'd have loved Bellaroo Creek. Both Krissie and Ty told a little story about their mum—even their dad. There wasn't a dry eye after that. They ended the service with a recording of Sarah's favourite song—the Hollies hit 'He Ain't Heavy, He's My Brother'.

A wake was held at the community hall. After refreshments and cake had been amply consumed, Tess strode up to the podium and called the room to order. 'Ty, Krissie and I wanted today to be a celebration of Sarah's life and you've all helped make that possible and I want to thank you from the bottom of my heart.'

Without any effort at all, she found Cam's tall broad bulk in the crowd. The smile he sent her warmed her to her toes. 'We miss Sarah every single day, but we don't want to focus any longer on all the bad stuff about missing her, but on how much better our lives are for having known her. Today, you helped us do that.'

She smoothed her hair back behind her ears. 'Something Ty, Krissie and I have taken to doing at dinnertime is naming something that has made us happy for that day or something that we're grateful for. Every single day I'm grateful that Sarah was my sister, but when she died I turned my back on my music. A very special guy here in Bellaroo Creek, though, showed me what a mistake that was. I'm very grateful to Cameron Manning for that lesson. I want to now play you all a piece that was one of my sister's favourites.'

She moved to the side where she'd stowed her guitar case and retrieved the guitar she'd had couriered from Sydney. She hadn't played it in over five months. She slipped the strap over her head, seated herself on a stool, and looked out at the sea of faces staring back at her. 'Sarah, honey, this one's for you,' she whispered.

She met Cam's eyes, drew in a breath at his encouraging nod, and then her fingers touched the strings and magic filled her. She lost herself to it, pouring her heart into the music.

When she finished she smiled at Ty and Krissie sitting on the floor in front of her. And then at Cam. He was right. The music was a gift, and there was room in her heart for it all—for Ty and Krissie, and for the music. She should embrace it.

'I want to invite anyone who'd like to take part, to come up here and share something that's made you happy or that you're grateful for.'

Cam stared in awe.

Tess Laing was the most amazing woman he'd ever met. If Bellaroo Creek could attract another couple of women with her spunk the town would be safe for the next hundred years. It wouldn't just be saved. It'd flourish!

Krissie walked up onto stage to the microphone. 'You should go down there now,' she whispered to Tess, pointing at the crowd, obviously not meaning for everyone to hear, but the microphone picking it up as Tess adjusted it for her.

With a kiss to the top of the child's head, Tess made her way down to the crowd to stand with Ty. Without consciously meaning to, Cam made his way to her side. She smiled at him, turning automatically as if she'd sensed him there. It made his gut clench.

Did he truly mean to leave this woman?

'I want to say that one thing that makes me happy is my auntie Tess. We do lots of fun things together like singing, and we dance around the backyard and colour-in together. She's not a very good dancer...'

Everyone laughed. Cam remembered seeing Tess dance and shook his head. She was a great dancer.

'But she's going to teach me guitar and I love living with her.'

He held Tess back when Krissie finished. 'Let her do it all under her own steam,' he counselled.

'I'm fussing, huh?'

He didn't interfere though when she bent down to encompass the child in a hug once Krissie had reached them. It wasn't until she righted herself, though, that he saw Ty had moved to the microphone.

'My auntie Tess is awesome, but today I want to say I'm happy Cam has been our neighbour. He's shown me how to stake tomato plants and how to nail chicken wire and how to teach Barney to fetch a ball. I'm going to miss him when he goes to Africa.'

There were a few 'hear, hears' from the crowd and Cam found his throat thickening. He lifted Ty up in a bear hug when he rejoined them. 'Thanks, buddy, I'm going to miss you too.'

'Me too?' Krissie tugged on his sleeve, demanding a hug of her own.

'You too,' he said, hugging her close.

Damn it! Did he really mean to leave these kids behind?

'Me three.' Tess leaned across and kissed his cheek. She backed up pretty quick again too, though, and he didn't blame her. Not if the heat threatened her in the same way it did him.

One by one the townsfolk walked up to the microphone to name the things that made them happy— family, a good wheat crop, a clean bill of health, family, friends who rallied around in times of need, good rainfall, grandchildren, family. *Family.* It figured high on everyone's happiness radar. Not a single person mentioned going to Africa—or any other place for that matter. Bellaroo Creek and family, that was what mattered.

Bellaroo Creek and family.

Cameron stared at Tess and the kids. Could he truly leave them? Did he *want* to leave them?

He stared at his mother. She'd miss him dreadfully. He knew that now, even if she was putting a brave face on it.

Family and Bellaroo Creek.

Lance and Fiona canoodled in a corner like the lovesick couple they were and he didn't even feel a pang. Instead he felt hopeful. Lance was keeping his word and working hard. Having finally emerged from under Cam's shadow, he was even showing some natural aptitude on the sheep-breeding programme. And it was obvious he had no intention of breaking Fiona's heart as Cam had feared.

Family and Bellaroo Creek.

Once upon a time that had been his dream too. When it had failed him he'd turned his back on it, proclaimed it impossible. His heart started to thump. But it wasn't impossible, was it? It was within reach if he had the courage to try for it.

He stared at Tess and Ty and Krissie, remembered

the laughter and light they'd brought to Kurrajong House, the life they'd sent flowing through it.

That dream of his wasn't impossible. Oh, it hadn't been possible with Fiona, and all he could do was be thankful that she'd realised it in time.

That dream of his was absolutely possible.

If only he wasn't too afraid to reach for it again.

His heart thundered in his ears. Tess had found the courage to embrace her music again. Could he find the same courage within himself?

He shoved his hands in his pockets and stared hard at the floorboards at his feet. What did he truly want? What would he lay his life down for and be glad to do it?

Tess.

That single word filled his soul.

'I'm next!' He pointed to the microphone. Everyone turned to stare at him. He swung to Tess, seized her face in his hands and kissed her soundly. His lips memorised every single curve and contour of hers and she kissed him back with such unguarded love it fed something essential inside him.

He let her go. He squeezed Krissie's and Ty's shoulders before striding up to the stage and the microphone.

Tess watched Cam adjust the microphone while the blood crashed through her veins.

He'd kissed her.

In front of everyone!

What did he mean by it?

Ty and Krissie grinned up at her. She couldn't help but grin back.

Cam cleared his throat. Her attention flew back to his tall frame and those powerful shoulders and lean hips...and long, long legs with their powerful thighs. Her knees quivered and her heart tripped and fluttered.

His gaze wandered about the crowd until she thought he must've made eye contact with everyone. 'I know every single one of you by your full name. I've listened to you recite the things that make you happy, the things that are most important to you, and the message has come through loud and clear—you love your families, your properties and Bellaroo Creek.'

He shifted. 'All I've ever wanted is to grow a big bustling family at Kurrajong Station, but a year ago that dream came crashing down around my ears and I thought it would never happen. That's when I made my decision to leave. I knew it would be too hard living here day in and day out with that dream mocking me.'

Her heart burned for all he'd been through.

'I want to say now that I'm grateful to Fiona for realising we weren't well suited and calling our engagement off before we made a dreadful mistake. I only wish I could've seen that truth sooner.'

He didn't love Fiona? Her hands clenched and unclenched until, to stop their fidgeting, she gripped them together.

'Because now I know what true love is.'

He did?

When his gaze moved to her, she had to press her hands to her heart to make sure it didn't leap right out of her chest.

'Loving someone means wanting them to be happy, even if it means giving up your own dreams. It means supporting them in the things that are important to them, even if you don't understand that importance.' He suddenly grinned. 'Like White Bearded Silkies and marigolds in a vegetable garden.'

Krissie tugged on Tess's blouse. 'Cam loves us, Auntie Tess.' She grinned as if it were the best news in the world.

'Course he does,' Ty scoffed, as if he'd always known as much.

She swallowed. Had she truly thought they wouldn't welcome another person into their lives? It was obvious that they'd welcome Cam.

Except...

Her heart started to wilt. Loving someone meant supporting their dreams. Cam's dream was to go to

Africa—to experience the world, to make a difference. She couldn't stand in the way of that.

'Loving someone means risking your heart, even if you've vowed to never do that again, even if you don't feel ready to take that leap.'

He was going to risk his heart for her, wasn't he? She wanted him to. Oh, how she wanted him to, but...

Africa. His dream.

'I want you all to know that I won't be going to Africa after all.'

Applause broke out along with several cheers. Tess couldn't bear to glance around. Her heart had slumped to her ankles.

'I'm going to fight for the life I want. I'm going to fight for my dream. If that dream proves impossible, I'm going to stay here in Bellaroo Creek anyway. I'm not going to turn my back on the town. This is where I belong.'

He climbed down from the stage and made his way directly to where she stood. Taking both Krissie's and Ty's hands, he led them away to the far side of the room and knelt down to speak to them. With his back to her she couldn't see what he said. She could only see the smiles that lit the children's faces, their decisive nods, and the hopeful glances they sent her way.

She wanted to close her eyes. She couldn't let him do this. When he rose and beckoned to her, she pulled in a breath and moved towards them. With a smile designed to heat her from the inside out, Cam took her hand. 'You guys go join the party again. Your aunt and I are going to talk.'

And with that he led her out of a side door and away from the noise of the hall until they stood beneath the fronds of a pepper tree that partially hid them from view. He stared down into her face, plucked one of the fronds from her hair, but he didn't say anything.

Loving someone means wanting them to be happy.

'When did you realise I'd fallen in love with you, Cameron?'

He touched her cheek with the backs of his fingers. He kept a firm grip on her hand. 'That day at my mother's.'

'It was the day I realised I loved you.' She paused and bit back a sigh. 'I don't think I'm very good at keeping things from you.'

His lips lifted. 'I'm glad about that.'

She gently detached her hand and moved a couple of steps back until she leant against the hard, rough trunk of the tree. He stiffened. 'I hope you mean to tell me what's troubling you now?'

Oh, how she would miss him!

Behind her, she closed her fingers about the rough bark. She dragged in a breath that hurt her lungs. 'All your life you've taken responsibility for other people. For your father when he cut himself off from the world, and for continuing his legacy in providing your mother with a haven if she should ever need it. For taking on the management of the property your stepfather left to her...and even for helping Lance find his feet. You help Edna and Ted Fairchild run cattle so they can stay in the home they love, and heaven only knows how many other people you help out in a similar way. You're amazing, Cameron, a true-blue hero. I swear I have yet to meet anyone with more decency and integrity.'

He adjusted his stance, legs wide and hands on hips, and her heart stuttered in her chest. 'Why, then,' he said, 'am I suddenly not happy to hear this?'

She ached to rush forward and throw her arms around his neck and tell him how much she loved him, but...

He deserved to chase his dreams.

'Because all your life you've taken on everyone else's responsibilities, but now you have a chance to travel and to find out where you truly want to be.'

'I know where I want to be.'

She wanted to believe him, but... 'Do you know how much responsibility it is raising two kids? Do you know how needy and...and...Cam, we—Ty, Krissie and me—we're *not* your responsibility.' She might not have given birth to Ty and Krissie, but they were hers now and she loved them as if she had.

'I know when you look at us you see a single mum with two kids who need rescuing, but—'

'Garbage!' He slashed a hand through the air, making her blink. 'I look at you, Tess, and I see an incredibly strong woman who manages to make me laugh even when I'm feeling my bleakest and grumpiest. I look at you and see a desirable woman I want to take to my bed and make love with thoroughly and comprehensively.'

She pressed hands to cheeks that burned.

He moved in close until all she could smell was the scent of cut grass and hot man, and all she could see was him.

'I look at you, Tess, and my soul sings and my heart is at rest and there's glitter in my world.'

He reached out to touch her face. 'I don't see a woman who needs rescuing. I see a woman with a safety net ready for me if I should ever fall. Tess, when I look at you I don't see a responsibility. I see my future. I see my soul mate. I see the woman I love.'

Her heart all but stopped.

His hands clenched, his eyes blazed with resolution. 'I don't know how long it will take me to convince you of the truth of that, but I want you to know I'm going to dedicate my life to doing exactly that.'

'But Africa,' she whispered. She wanted him happy. She wanted him to follow his dream.

'To hell with Africa! It was my consolation prize.

I'm not running away. I'm not leaving Bellaroo Creek. And let me tell you another thing.' He jabbed a finger at her nose. 'I'm not making way for some other single farmer to make a move on you.' He thrust out his jaw. 'I'm not going anywhere!'

She stared at him. He stared back, his eyes a glowing, gleaming green. 'Africa is not where I want to be. Wherever you are, Tess, that's where I'm going to make my home—whether that be at Kurrajong House, your little farmhouse or in Sydney.'

He meant it. Every single word.

And she could see the exact moment when he clocked her belief in him. His smile was like drought-ridden land coming back to life after vital rain.

He reached out to cup her face. 'Your eyes tell me you're going to say yes when I ask you to marry me.'

She grinned. She couldn't help it. She reached up to touch his cheek, before moving in closer to wind her arms about his neck. 'Yours tell me you've already asked for the children's permission.'

'They gave it gladly.'

Of course they had. They adored Cam as much as she did. 'My eyes don't lie, Cameron. I love you. My heart is completely and utterly yours.'

Just as his was hers. And she meant to treasure it and keep it safe for ever.

He stared down at her as if her words were magic. She moved against him suggestively. 'So, what do you mean to do with your Bellaroo Creek bride once you have her?'

His head dipped towards her, blocking out the sun. 'I mean to make her the happiest woman on the planet,' he murmured against her lips, before he captured them in a kiss of such pure joy Tess felt as if she were flying and swooping among the treetops.

* * * * *

COMING NEXT MONTH from Harlequin® Romance
AVAILABLE AUGUST 6, 2013

#4387 THE COWBOY SHE COULDN'T FORGET
Slater Sisters of Montana
Patricia Thayer

Ana Slater knows she can't look after her ranch alone. Her only hope is the cowboy she has found it impossible to forget—Vance Rivers.

#4388 A MARRIAGE MADE IN ITALY
Rebecca Winters

Leon Malatesta is fiercely protective of his baby daughter. But does Belle Peterson's arrival bring the possibility of a new future for all of them?

#4389 MIRACLE IN BELLAROO CREEK
Bellaroo Creek
Barbara Hannay

Ed Cavanaugh always knew Milla Brady deserved true love. So when he arrives in Bellaroo Creek, he resolves to tell her how he truly feels....

#4390 THE COURAGE TO SAY YES
Barbara Wallace

Abby Gray needs a fresh start to finally put the past behind her. Can Hunter Smith convince her that happy-ever-afters do happen in real life?

You can find more information on upcoming Harlequin® titles, free excerpts and more at www.Harlequin.com.

LARGER-PRINT BOOKS!

GET 2 FREE LARGER-PRINT NOVELS PLUS
2 FREE GIFTS!

HARLEQUIN®

Romance

From the Heart, For the Heart

YES! Please send me 2 FREE LARGER-PRINT Harlequin® Romance novels and my 2 FREE gifts (gifts are worth about $10). After receiving them, if I don't wish to receive any more books, I can return the shipping statement marked "cancel." If I don't cancel, I will receive 4 brand-new novels every month and be billed just $4.84 per book in the U.S. or $5.24 per book in Canada. That's a savings of at least 19% off the cover price! It's quite a bargain! Shipping and handling is just 50¢ per book in the U.S. and 75¢ per book in Canada.* I understand that accepting the 2 free books and gifts places me under no obligation to buy anything. I can always return a shipment and cancel at any time. Even if I never buy another book, the two free books and gifts are mine to keep forever.

119/319 HDN F43Y

Name _____ (PLEASE PRINT) _____

Address _____ Apt. # _____

City _____ State/Prov. _____ Zip/Postal Code _____

Signature (if under 18, a parent or guardian must sign)

Mail to the **Harlequin® Reader Service:**
IN U.S.A.: P.O. Box 1867, Buffalo, NY 14240-1867
IN CANADA: P.O. Box 609, Fort Erie, Ontario L2A 5X3

Want to try two free books from another line?
Call 1-800-873-8635 or visit www.ReaderService.com.

* Terms and prices subject to change without notice. Prices do not include applicable taxes. Sales tax applicable in N.Y. Canadian residents will be charged applicable taxes. Offer not valid in Quebec. This offer is limited to one order per household. Not valid for current subscribers to Harlequin Romance Larger-Print books. All orders subject to credit approval. Credit or debit balances in a customer's account(s) may be offset by any other outstanding balance owed by or to the customer. Please allow 4 to 6 weeks for delivery. Offer available while quantities last.

ANA NEVER WAS one to take risks. She was the oldest, the sensible daughter. She always tried to do the right thing. So why was she walking across the compound to Vance's house just before dawn? She was afraid to even answer that question. She was shaking as she walked up the steps, then before she could chicken out, she knocked on the door. She stood there a few minutes and almost felt relieved when there wasn't an answer. Just as she started to leave, the door opened and Vance stood there wearing only a pair of jeans and a towel draped around his neck.

Oh, God. She loved looking at this man. She met his eyes and tried desperately to speak, but nothing came out of her mouth.

He reached for her, pulled her into the house and closed the door, pushing her back against it. A soft light came from over the stove in the kitchen, letting her see the look of desire in his eyes.

"What are you doing here?"

"I didn't like how we left things last night."

"So you thought coming here just before dawn was a wise thing to do?"

"I couldn't sleep."

"Join the club, lady. You've kept invading my dreams ever since you've come back home."

His honesty shocked her. "Really?"

In answer, he lowered his head and covered her mouth with his. With a soft moan, she gripped his bare arms, feeling his strength. Yet he held her with tenderness as he placed teasing kisses against her lips.

"We could bring my dreams to life if you like," he told her before he gave her another sample. He captured her mouth in a deep kiss, causing her knees to give out.

He wrapped his arms around her, pulling her close. "I got you," he whispered.

She laid her head against his chest, feeling his rapid heartbeat. "I've always wanted you, Vance," she breathed.

THE COWBOY SHE COULDN'T FORGET
by Patricia Thayer is available August 2013 only from Harlequin® Romance.